D0458936

THE RAINBOW KITE

THE RAINBOW KITE

MARLENE FANTA SHYER

MARSHALL CAVENDISH • NEW YORK

Marshall Cavendish, 99 White Plains Road, Tarrytown, NY 10591

Library of Congress Cataloging-in-Publication Data
Shyer, Marlene Fanta.
The rainbow kite / by Marlene Fanta Shyer.
p. cm.
Summary: Twelve-year-old Matthew describes the prejudices and struggles that his entire family faces when people learn that his older brother Bennett is gay.
ISBN 0-7614-5122-6
[1. Homosexuality—Fiction. 2. Prejudices—fiction. 3. Brother—Fiction. 4. Fathers and sons—fiction.] I. Title.
PZ7.S562 Rai 2002
[Fic]—dc21
2001053894

The text of this book is set in 12 point Caslon 540.
Book design by Constance Ftera
Printed in the United States of America
First edition
1 3 5 6 4 2

To Chris –

also

to the boys and girls of the Hommocks School

and a special thank you to James Norell

THE RAINBOW KITE

1

There was a storm that night, but it wasn't rain or thunder that woke me. It was my brother crying. I sat right up in bed, scared down to my bones. I hadn't heard Bennett cry since he was twelve, I was about to be ten, and Frankie died. That was over two years ago. Frankie was very old and died of a shot the vet gave him when he could hardly move or bark or recognize us anymore, and it took me all of fall and winter to get over it. In a way, I guess Bennett never did.

"What is it?" I whispered to my brother. At first I thought bad dreams or appendicitis. I knew a kid who had to have his taken out and he said the pain was like two knives and a fork jabbing him in his right side.

"What?" My brother's voice was froggy, like coming from a swamp.

"You're crying," I said.

"I'm not. You're dreaming. Just go back to sleep," Bennett said.

But he couldn't kid me. I thought it was one of the worst sounds I'd ever heard.

Next morning, it was business as usual. My mother looking for her keys because she misplaces things all the time, my father complaining about his shoulder, on hold with the airport, trying to see if his plane was leaving on time. He's a salesman of office furniture and sometimes gets a pain from carrying his laptop and a whole bunch of catalogs in his black case. My mother does private nursing, which means she works some days and not others. Sometimes she's even gone weekends.

But that morning, she was making English muffins with eggs on top and talking about a patient she was on her way to take care of, a Mrs. Dowd who couldn't get things right anymore and always called Mom "Sis." My mother's name is Lydia, but Dad calls her Lyd, except when she misplaces his newspaper or the telephone message pad. "You'd lose your teeth, Lydia, if they weren't stuck in your gums," he'll mutter, sort of over-easy, but when he gets mad at us, it's different. It's not a pretty sight. When Bennett quit Little League, Dad slapped the wall so hard he had to take a pill for his shoulder and couldn't shoot baskets with me for a week.

When my brother came down to breakfast that morning, I could see whatever it was was still in there, living its own life behind his eyes. He just wouldn't look at me. He was staring out the window as if there was a video playing outside and he didn't want to miss a second of it. Otherwise, nothing happening. He ate two muffins and burped real loud in two keys, which is what he thinks is funny. "Excuse *me*," Mom said, and Dad gave him a dark look and asked if he'd practiced swim laps yesterday and for how long and was he increasing his speed? And then he looked my way and remembered the saxophone. "One hour, no less, Matthew!"

Ever since Dad bought it for me, he's been after me to practice every day. He said he'd played in a school band when he was a kid and it was a wholesome experience. Dad is very into wholesome experiences. Mostly they fall into the category of things nobody likes to do, like when I had to spend two weeks with Grandpa at a retirement community after Grandma died, and Bennett's having to paint part of the house every year. Most important, we must *never, never quit anything we start.*

Dad slaps walls when we begin something and don't finish. He thinks if you start a project, a sport, or a musical instrument, you have to carry it through maybe right until you get old enough to be on two canes and eat soft food.

I've been playing alto sax for two years now because I started when I didn't know any better and am now doomed to blow into it for as long as I have breath in my body. *Stick with it!* That's Dad's motto, and he's not letting us forget it.

The problem is that although Bennett is pretty good at everything, after Frankie died he could never stick with *anything.*

He had a picture of Frankie pasted up over his bed and another framed on his dresser and once I saw him reach over and touch the one over his bed as if he were trying to pet the photograph. Frankie was definitely Bennett's dog and wherever Bennett was, there was Frankie right next to him. Once when my brother was sick with the flu, Mom tried to keep him in the kitchen so Bennett would get a good night's sleep. Frankie was up all night long. It seemed he couldn't so much as close his eyes if he didn't get carried up to the top bunk to sleep at the foot of my brother's bed.

We have some puppy pictures of him when both ears were still flapped down, but the funny thing was that only one ear managed to wobble up and the other stayed flopped over like it didn't have the stamina for standing. It was that way for the rest of his life. Bennett said Frankie was a state-of-the-art dog, with a solid gold canine heart. "Smart! I could teach him to read if I wanted to," Bennett claimed, and I almost believed him.

I think it was the ear thing that convinced Bennett that there was something one-of-a-kind about Frankie. "Ever see a dog with one up and one down in your whole entire life?"

Nobody had.

"See? He's just not like a regular dog. He's one in a million."

"Okay, he's irregular, then," Dad said.

"That's it," Bennett said. "He's irregular, like me."

A few months after Frankie died, Bennett quit ice hockey. He gave me his skates and stick. "Hockey just doesn't ring up my curtain," he said, and that's when Dad bought him a goatskin catcher's glove and offered to get us a new dog.

Bennett flat-out wasn't having any new dog. Even the idea made him mad, he said. It was disloyal! As if another dog could replace Frankie! What he said shocked Mom. "If Matthew died, would you get me a new brother to replace *him*?" Dad said the remark was out of order, but he'd made his position clear. So, even though I wanted a puppy, Bennett overruled. Nobody wanted to upset him any more than he was already. I think Dad and Mom were afraid he'd just stop going to school, even stop *breathing*.

He didn't, but the night after I heard him crying, he put his whole dog and cat stamp collection in an old Christmas box at the back of his closet and tied it up with a couple of old hockey skate shoelaces tied in fancy knots. I figured that was it; he was quitting the Stamp and Coin Club. "Why?" I asked him. "Just doesn't grease my wheels," he said, and that was a puzzler. I thought he really liked that club. He had dog and cat stamps from all over the world he sometimes traded with other members. He said the stamps were his most valuable possession and he would never part with them. Like they were some kind of rare treasures, he'd put them into these little envelopes with tweezers and wouldn't let anyone near them, especially me.

He quit Little League even before the first real game. He used the new goatskin catcher's glove about *twice.* When Dad turned blossom pink and smacked the wall, my brother decided to join the swim team. He'd won a ribbon at Boy Scout Camp and could race on his back, his front, or his side. He could keep his feet straight as sticks when he kicked, too, which I never could seem to, and hold his breath under water longer than the coach. But, I could tell that although he'd already pinned two medals on his bulletin board, by the way he talked about the meets he was just hanging in to make Dad happy.

The thing was, Bennett was alone a lot. He had only two friends. One was Shearon, his elementary school buddy, but Shearon was black and now seemed to prefer his African-American friends to Bennett. The other was Moira, but she stopped coming around when she got a boyfriend who took up all her time. Sometimes when I thought about it, Shearon and Moira's seemed like lame excuses. It was as if Bennett was sending out invisible vibes that kept kids away.

When a new family moved next door, Mom and Dad jumped right in and invited them over for Sunday night supper because the youngest kid in the family was Bennett's age. I remember it pretty well. Dad had set up a new basketball hoop in the driveway and Bennett and me and the kid, whose name is Terry, shot some baskets. Later we sat at our kitchen table and ate hamburgers together and then Bennett and Terry went inside and played a video game while I helped Dad clean up. That was the last time Terry ever came over to our place. Right away he got a ton of new friends, kids Bennett knew from the neighborhood; you could hear them next door every day after school, hanging out in Terry's yard.

"Maybe Bennett just likes to be alone," I heard Mom say to Dad once, when they didn't know I was listening.

"He's irregular, all right, Lyd." I heard the worry in Dad's voice. "God, I wish I knew what makes the kid tick."

2

That same morning, Dad left for Boston on the shuttle flight. He said he'd be home by eight and by that time, he hoped to see some progress on the Sousa march I've been practicing on the sax and my Social Studies report on global hunger. Mom was rushing around, looking for her scarf, her car keys and her gasoline credit card. I saw Bennett stuff an extra bunch of brownies in his backpack when Mom wasn't looking, and then he and I ran for the school bus.

As soon as it started rolling, I reminded Bennett he had promised like five times to give me the goatskin catcher's glove. A couple of the guys and I like to play softball Saturdays and my old one was getting way too small. When Bennett quit Little League, he lent the gorgeous oil-tanned, hinge-back glove Dad had bought him to his friend who wasn't really his friend anymore, Shearon. Shearon plays softball in a league across town.

"You'll get it soon, Matthew," Bennett said, which is what he always tells me, and he put on his earphones, turned on his Walkman, and tuned me out.

"When's soon gonna be?" I asked, but he'd brought his Nirvana tape and didn't hear me.

I was busy in school that day helping make posters for International Brotherhood Week and checking out the set of triplets who just transferred to our school from

Chicago, Illinois. The DeWitts looked pretty much alike except for one, Nolan, whose hair was a little darker than the others', sort of like the shade of the brownies in Bennett's backpack.

I guess I had brownies on my mind. I had just finished my tuna-and-egg sandwiches and my one and only brownie at lunch. They are not your everyday baked goods but thick, fat, almost-like-candy-bars Mom sometimes picks up at the bakery near Mrs. Dowd's house. I decided I wanted another one and went looking for my brother in the cafeteria, figuring he'd share his. He'd grabbed at least six more than I had out of the bakery box on the top cupboard shelf—where I couldn't reach.

When I located him, there were a bunch of guys sitting all around him, which was really unusual. Most of the time, if I don't sit with him, Bennett is alone, usually at the end of a long table not far from the cashier. I sometimes think the cashier is the only one in the lunchroom who talks to him.

As soon as I got to his table, though, I saw that getting a brownie from my brother was not going to happen. No wonder Bennett was surrounded! He was doling them out to the guys.

"Hey, Bennett! What are you doing that for?" I admit I was ticked. My mouth was ready for a brownie and now it looked like I was out of luck. He was distributing them and not to me. "Hey, Bennett!" I started to yell at him, but remembered last night, the sound of his middle-of-the-night crying, and I backed off.

My brother was acting like he didn't hear me and that's when it hit home. For once, he had lots of company and it looked like he'd given away every single brownie, even his own. And although he knew he was going to get it later from Mom for taking all those extras, I guessed having friends to sit with at lunch was worth it all to him.

Nolan and I sat next to each other in computer class and he told me there were even more kids in his family: a sister in high school and an older brother who was the same age as Bennett. "He's real short," Nolan told me, and then he whispered that in Chicago this undersized brother, Jeremy, used to hang from a pole he put up in a doorway so he'd stretch out and get longer. I told him my brother was a little offbeat too, although Bennett is tall enough—at least a head taller than I am. "What's the matter with *him*?" Nolan wanted to know, but what could I say? I didn't want to say "irregular," I didn't want to tell him my brother has to give out brownies to make friends. "He's sort of great at everything he does but then he doesn't do it," I told him.

Anyway, Nolan said he'd come over after school to help me prepare the Power Point Presentation on global hunger. He said he could do graphics on the PC faster than the speed of light. It was because he was the oldest triplet—by twelve minutes—and therefore the smartest by twelve IQ points. Unfortunately, when he arrived at my house, Nolan said he'd never seen a PC like ours, couldn't figure out our software, and couldn't work out my pie chart.

So Nolan and I headed out to the driveway with my basketball, and that's when things began to unfold.

Shearon came pedaling down our driveway, looking for

Bennett, but my brother hadn't come home from school yet. I remembered he'd gone to a swim meet. "When's he gonna be here?" Shearon wanted to know. I guessed about an hour or so, so we stayed out and Shearon joined in shooting baskets for a while, and would have put both Nolan and me to shame, only he wasn't concentrating. He kept missing easy shots, telling us he preferred volleyball any day of the week and looking at his watch. He kept checking the road to see if Bennett was coming.

"What do you want Bennett for anyways?" It was Nolan who asked, not me, right after Shearon had made his first really good shot. I hadn't seen Shearon here in a long time and was wondering the same thing.

"I want to borrow his glove. Mine, it was brand new, I stuck it in my backpack and somebody just reached in and swiped it." Shearon was watching the ball hit the rim and bounce through the basket. "Let me tell you, I was pretty perturbed."

"*Perturbed?*" Nolan said.

"It's an eighth-grade vocabulary word," Shearon explained, throwing the ball to me. You never know what's going to come out of him next, which is one reason my brother likes him. "So that's why I need Bennett's glove for a while, capeesh?"

I just dribbled the ball, thinking Shearon probably forgot he still *had* Bennett's glove. "Bennett says you've got it," I told him after I said, "Good shot."

"You're kidding, right? I gave it back two weeks ago. After me, he lent it to Go-go Mallis."

Go-go was one of the guys eating Mom's brownies at lunch. He's the unofficial king of our school, and not because he's that smart or a top athlete. He's king because he looks like he could wrestle a dinosaur with his left hand and win, cuts at least one class every week, and mostly because he once brought six mice to school and let them run through Mrs. Warren's Language Arts class. Ever since Go-go hid Bennett's gym uniform in a hall trash basket, I always thought Bennett didn't much go for Go-go.

Besides, he'd promised the glove to me!

I didn't know what to say, so I asked Shearon if he wanted to come inside and have a cold drink. Mom's car had just pulled in the driveway. I was thirsty and we could wait for Bennett in the kitchen.

"Sure, why not?" Shearon said, and he added, "Yeah, I gave your brother his glove in the cafeteria Friday before last. Then Go-go came by and asked if he could have it. I think your brother is always trying to get on Go-go's good side. Problem is Go-go doesn't have a good side."

"So Bennett let Go-go have it?"

"Let's say Go-go *appropriated* it. That's another eighth-grade vocabulary word. It means he *helped himself to it*, but Go-go swore he gave it back a couple of days ago."

We all went inside and right away Mom went for the brownies. The funny thing was that she'd sort of lost track of how many there were supposed to be left and I quickly said, "Bennett and I took a couple extra," so she wouldn't think about counting, and she let it go, maybe because we had company. She pulled out some milk and a box of doughnut holes she'd stashed in the refrigerator.

Nolan said his older brother once made a tower of doughnut holes, glued them together, sprayed them gold and turned them into a Christmas tree. His brother could build anything, and built a pair of stilts for himself and right now he was building a kite that would look just like the American flag. Shearon did not seem to be interested in hearing about Nolan's brother, and kept staring at the clock over the refrigerator.

When my brother finally came walking in, he still looked sort of droopy, but his face lit up when he saw Shearon. "Hey, Shear, where you been?" he asked.

"I been real busy," Shearon answered, and I could see Mom watching his face and figured out right away what I did: Shearon looked like someone real busy making up excuses. "Actually, I just came to ask a favor, Ben-boy."

Bennett sat down at the table and I introduced him to Nolan. Mom put a glass of milk in front of everybody.

"So. What's the favor?"

"It's the glove you lent me. Could I borrow it again?"

Bennett shot me a quick glance, maybe hoping I didn't hear this. I did, though, and kept my eye on him the whole time Shearon was telling him the story of how his brand new glove that he'd saved a year for, came to be stolen out of his backpack.

"It's not here, the glove," Bennett said.

"It's not?" Shearon looked unbelievably disappointed, but not so disappointed that he stopped munching and sipping.

"No, it's not."

My brother had a milk mustache now and looked like

one of those magazine ads for the milk industry. I was thinking *Something is fishy here.*

"Why didn't you tell me Go-go had it?" I asked.

Bennett had a funny look and it wasn't the milk mustache. "You'll get it, Matthew." I know when Bennett's coming down with something and this seemed like one of those times. What it was he was coming down with, I didn't know.

"So, where is it now?" Nolan asked, altogether innocent about everything going on at our kitchen table. He was digging in for another doughnut hole, his mouth still full of the last one.

"It's in my locker. At school," Bennett said.

Shearon seemed relieved. "So Go-go did give it back to you. Great. Then, could you let me have it for a couple of weeks? I'll be real careful with it. No backpacks! I could meet you at the lockers, say third period?"

"Can't do that, Shear. Sorry," Bennett said.

"You can't? Why not?"

"I promised it to my little brother here, didn't I, Matthew?"

I wished he would stop calling me his little brother and I've told him that like a thousand times, but, "Yes, he did," I said. "He did promise."

"Oh boy. Well, I better go look somewhere else, then," Shearon said, not moving, looking ready to put his head right on the table and cry. "So how come you didn't tell me that soon as I got here?" I was wondering the same thing. And I was wondering why if Bennett's glove was in his locker, he hadn't given it to me long ago.

Nolan's mouth was still pretty full, but that didn't stop him jumping right in and saving the day.

"Hey, my older brother has a glove he never uses. He'll lend you the glove, sure as anything."

"No kidding," Shearon said, lighting up.

Nolan's mouth was very full. "Oh, sure. He won't mind," he said, and gave Shearon his address.

Shearon gave Nolan a high five. "I'll come by tomorrow then, okay?"

"Not tomorrow. It's Saturday and we're all helping Dad clean up the cellar. Come by Monday, okay?"

"You're not busy tomorrow, Shearon?" Bennett quickly piped up. "Why don't you come by here? We could hang out. Maybe ride our bikes to the beach, Or, I got a new Nirvana tape and a video of a guy bungee jumping off the highest cliff in the Grand Canyon—"

"Isn't there a swim meet tomorrow?" I asked my brother. I remember seeing the big red circle on my mother's kitchen calendar and thought of going myself, to see Bennett help our team beat Whitney Young Junior High.

"There's a swim meet, but I won't be there," Bennett announced, like it was nothing. "I'm quitting the team."

"You *are*?" I wondered if quitting swimming had anything to do with his crying last night. I was dead sure I hadn't imagined it, the way it was still ringing in my ears.

I also wondered what Dad would say and why Bennett would quit a sport I thought he really liked.

For the moment though, the number one mystery of the glove was the big issue, and the major cliff hanger for me.

3

"Why did you let Go-go take your glove?" I asked my brother as soon as the guys had left. He was heading up to the room in our house that's Dad's office, two steps at a time. That's where we keep our computer and that's where we get into fights about whose turn it is to use it. Bennett likes playing games like Chromo Cross and Bleem and my favorite, Neo Geo, which is why he always keeps the door closed. Whenever he hears Dad on the stairs, I happen to know he pushes the mouse to X and pretends he's working on a school project.

"Bennett! Why did you do it? You promised it to me!" I kept after him, my voice going louder every step, but Bennett never really gave me a good answer. He told me not to worry; I'd get it sooner or later. "Anyway, Go-go messed it up and I gotta clean it up first. Okay?"

The door closed. I was standing out in the hall, and let me tell you, I was really steamed. To tell the truth, I felt like slapping the wall myself.

The day we buried our dog was the day I saw my brother really fall apart. When Dad brought him home from the vet's, Frankie looked like he was sleeping and would wake up any minute and want to play. Dad wrapped him in one of the bags we use for the falling leaves we have to rake up every year around September and October, then Bennett and I watched him put Frankie in a big cardboard box with his collar and leash and surround his body with rocks. I don't even know where Dad got them, but there they were, around four or five big ones, tucked all around. Dad put on sunglasses although it was not very sunny that day, but I think it was because he didn't want the world, especially us, to see his eyes tearing up. Mom said she wouldn't go with us when we laid him to rest. She was the one who had rescued Frankie from the pound the year Bennett was born, picked him out of umpteen puppies, because she said she could see that he was the one dog above all the others that had a soul. She named him after her favorite singer. "I can't go, I'm sorry," she said.

So Dad and Bennett and I and the body of Frankie (Dad put the box in another leaf bag and tied it with a heavy cord) drove out to Edgewater Point. It was autumn and I remember seeing pumpkins on doorsteps when we drove through the streets of town. I thought back to the Halloween two years before when a couple of tough guys had grabbed my bags of candy and just took off. Bennett and Frankie chased them down a block away until they dropped the bags and flew off, scared to death. Now Bennett said, "No way I'm ever going out on Hallowe'en without Frankie again," and in fact, after that he never did put on a mask, wear a costume or go trick-or-treating with me again.

I guess that's how he thought about Frankie, maybe not only as his best friend, but as his guardian angel too.

At Edgewater Point, we walked onto the fishing bridge that stretches out over the water and when we passed the old tackle shop next to it, for some reason I noticed there was a whole bunch of gulls on the roof. I thought they were just sitting and waiting for us to do what we had to do, like a row of witnesses. Dad stopped for a minute and just stood there, holding the box with Frankie in it, and he looked down at the water, which looked dark and cold. "Okay, guys, let's say a quiet prayer," he said, and we all just thought a prayer because maybe we were all too embarrassed to speak one out. We knew we wouldn't be able to get the words pronounced without breaking up, so we got all quiet and stood there for a few minutes, not looking at each other.

Then Dad leaned over the bridge and he dropped the box over the side, and he said, "Oh, God, Frankie, we're going to miss you," and he was going to say more, but his voice just got stuck down in his throat when the box was swallowed by the water. I tried to figure out how deep it was and how long it would take Frankie to reach the bottom.

And then I was behind Bennett running back to the car, and his shoulders were shaking, and that was the last time I heard my brother really let go—stretched out in the back seat going home—and it was awful, that sobbing sound, the worst I'd ever heard. Until last night.

Dad got home later than expected, it was way after dinner, and he said he'd had a really hard day but was not too tired to listen to me practice, although looking over my global hunger report could wait until Sunday. He wanted to see if I'd mastered the Sousa march. Since I'd only given it ten minutes after dinner, I got ready for the usual lecture, and Dad didn't disappoint me. Bennett calls it one of his We Must Strive talks.

"You may think I'm being too hard on you," he began, and I could have recited the rest right along with him. About how he'd goofed up in high school and barely made it into a state college, and how important it was to get into a fine university so we'd have the opportunities he'd never had, scholarships maybe, and so on. He'd had to drop out of school because his father left the family to go to Argentina and never sent back so much as a post-card. Dad doesn't like being a salesman that much, which is all he is qualified to do. He finished off with the usual, "I'm here, I'm not in Argentina, and I know I'm pushing you but I promise you'll thank me later."

"How much later?" I asked, but not until he'd gone upstairs and couldn't hear me.

I didn't really want to be around when Bennett told him he was quitting the swim team, so I practiced a while and then went up to my room and closed the door. Pretty soon, Bennett came up too. "What did Dad say?" I asked my brother.

"About what?"

"About you quitting the swim team."

"I'll break the news tomorrow," Bennett said.

"You mean, you haven't told him?"

"After breakfast. I'll tell him after breakfast."

"Why'd you want to quit anyway, Ben?" I asked.

"I guess swimming just doesn't put any wind in my sails," Bennett said, and I remember thinking, not in a million years will I ever understand my brother.

4

Dad makes special cinnamon French toast on Saturdays and I could hardly eat mine. I kept watching Bennett to see if he was ready to break the news and noticed he wasn't eating either. In fact, he looked as if he'd already had too much breakfast and might be getting ready to be sick.

"What's wrong with you guys?" Dad asked, standing at the stove, with that steel shovel thing he uses to flip the toast beginning to look like a weapon in his hand. Of course, that was just my imagination. Dad was looking goofy in one of Mom's ladylike aprons and I guess I can read his moods pretty well. It was an all-smiles one. Mom was making coffee and talking to one of her telephone friends at the same time, and everything looked cheery. Then, when Bennett put down his fork and said he couldn't eat, I could practically feel the air around my head sizzle.

"Are you sick?" Dad wanted to know. Mom put her hand over the receiver and came to attention.

"No," Bennett answered, looking down at his plate of French toast as if a worm had crawled across it.

"You're nervous about the meet." I thought Dad looked ready to give Bennett a We Must Strive talk.

Bennett didn't answer. Mom told whoever was on the line that she'd call back later, and put the receiver back into its cradle. "What's wrong, Bennett?" she asked.

When Bennett answered, "I'm quitting the swim team," I thought Dad would throw the flipper thing right at him. I was afraid I'd personally have to duck because if the utensil came flying I was directly in the path. But Dad just stood with the weapon suspended in the air over the frying pan and stared at Bennett as if he'd never laid eyes on him before. "Really?" he said, his voice deeper than a baritone sax. "*Really?* And may I ask *why?*"

Bennett knew better than to give Dad the sort of wiseass replies I was used to getting. Instead, he just shrugged.

Then Dad slammed the flipper down against the stove and turned red around the eyes. He looked at Bennett as if he was going to come over and do a few karate chops on him, but instead, Mom rushed over and put one hand on each of my brother's cheeks and looked down into his eyes and I guess tried to read what was going on in there, back in my brother's head. "Why, Bennett? You are such a strong swimmer!"

No answer from my brother. He picked up his fork and turned it upside down and right side up and just wouldn't look at anybody, even Mom.

"A *reason!*" Dad yelled. He was moving towards Bennett, but I was happy to see he had put down the weapon. "I need a *reason*!" he yelled. He did not slap a wall because there was really no wall handy. The kitchen is all cluttered with appliances and a window and stuff. That didn't stop Dad from slapping the table right in front of Bennett's plate. His glass of milk shook and I thought it was going to tip right over, but it just jumped a little, and so did Bennett. He stopped playing with the fork and looked at Dad and burst out with, "I hate the swim team!" and he leaped out of his chair and ran upstairs. Dad ran right after him.

I heard my father's voice booming from upstairs a minute later but couldn't hear exactly what he was saying. I only heard a few words that I could identify from another one of his We Must Strive lectures. And of course, I heard the word, "Argentina." I heard my brother's voice too, but it sounded very small and far away.

Mom sat down across the table from me and poured a little extra syrup on my French toast and asked me please to try to eat some and the next thing there was the smell of smoke; the toast on the stove was burning. Mom jumped up and turned off the gas jets and opened a window and then sat down opposite me at the table and shook her head and asked if I knew what was Bennett's problem. For the moment, I thought Bennett's problem was Dad, but what could I say?

"He's just not like other guys," I told her, which of course she knew. I didn't mention his crying. I didn't want to upset her anymore than she was already. "I don't know what's so great about the swim team, anyway," I said, and I tried, really tried, to get a few chunks of toast past my mouth and down into my stomach.

A few minutes later, my brother and father came walking down the stairs. My father's hand was on my brother's shoulder and it looked more as if he was maneuvering him than as if Bennett was walking of his own free will. "We're compromising on this, Lyd," Dad said. "Bennett is going to go to meet this afternoon. He's going to swim for his team. My son is not a quitter. He's not going to let his school down; he's going to follow through."

Bennett was looking down at his sneakers so I couldn't see his face. He certainly had nothing to say for the moment.

"And we're all going down to the gym to see his team beat Whitney Young Junior High!" Dad added, and he pulled off Mom's apron, bunched it up in his hands and threw it on the chair Bennett had been sitting in. "Okay, guys?" he asked, looking at Mom.

My mother nodded and I know her moods too. She looked like she looks at the end of a day, when she's tired and her feet really hurt. "Okay," she said. "We'll all go."

5

I always wished I could swim like my brother. I actually tried out for the team, but it took me about twice as long to get from one side of the pool to the other as any of the other kids. So, whenever I see my brother dive into the water and glide his way across the pool like he was born a fish, I admit I get a little envious.

Today's meet was a one hundred meter freestyle swim. Mom, Dad,and I were sitting in the bleachers and I was inhaling the smell of chlorine, which I love. It's not that he can't do a butterfly or backstroke, but freestyle happens to be Bennett's strongest stroke, so it was a sure bet he was going to help pull the team to victory. The starting pistol went off, the guys dove in, but the race was not that interesting at first. It was a relay and our team was ahead. I was thinking I could have been at the softball field out there on second base instead of watching the inevitable here, when suddenly a kid from Whitney Young dove in and swam so fast you could have sworn he was motorized. The weird thing about this kid was that he'd put nail polish on his toenails in his team colors. No one could miss him with his blue and yellow toenails. Now all of a sudden their team was ahead, there was lots of screaming, and their coach was running back and forth yelling things into the water and waving his arms.

Finally, when it looked like Whitney Young was going

to be the winner, my brother dove into the pool. He was the freestyle star of the team and the coach always let him go last, to pull us ahead. I could see Dad was sitting at the edge of his seat and Mom was too. She was biting one of her fingernails—her pinkie—and trying to look calm. Go-go and his crowd were in the row in front of us, cheering louder than anybody.

At first, Bennett raced ahead. The way his arms propelled in and out of the water, the way his legs scissored, you knew you were looking at a headliner. "Go!" everyone was yelling. "Go, go, go!" Kids were chanting, and the crowd was roaring. Dad stood up and then so did Mom, raising both arms in the air and shouting with the rest. "Go, Bennett, go!"

And Bennett went on, jetting through the water, gaining on the guy in the next lane, then passing him. The crowd was screaming, there were whistles and stomping and then, just as he was about to reach the far end of the pool, just as it was beginning to feel like our team winning was a sure thing, Bennett stopped dead in the water. He came to a dead halt as if his arms and legs had forgotten what to do. With his head and half his body sticking up out of the water at the shallow end, my brother was frozen in place, looking as if he were just a cardboard cutout of himself standing in a blue lake.

For a second, the crowd was still. I suppose everyone thought some terrible thing had happened. Dad's face went white and Mom went sinking into her seat with both hands over her mouth. A moment later, though, after the last swimmer from Whitney Young had reached the edge of the pool, the whistle blew, and the winners began lifting themselves out of the water, Bennett dog-paddled himself to the edge of the pool, pulled himself out, and sat dripping there on the cement ledge, knocking water out of one of his ears. The coach came over to him right away and we couldn't hear what he was saying, but my brother kept rubbing his leg, the part between the knee and the ankle, and we watched the coach lean over to look at it. Mom and Dad were up and making their way through the bleachers to get to him too. A few of my friends were yelling at me, "What happened to your brother?" and "What's up?" "Is he sick?" but I ignored them.

It was a cramp that had stopped him, my brother later explained, and Dad said that these things happen, and not to feel bad about it. At least Bennett had tried, Dad went on, and had put in a good effort, was to be commended, but my father sounded as if the steam had gone out of him. I don't think he really deep down believed Bennett, and neither did I.

I followed my brother to the locker room to make sure he took the glove out of his locker to give me and noticed that he stopped limping as soon as he was out of everyone's sight. The other guys never said a word to him, but a few were throwing looks his way and muttering things under their breath. I heard one comment that Bennett heard too: "What do you expect from a three-letter man?" but I didn't know what they were talking about, not then.

I was too upset anyway, because Bennett wouldn't let me come with him to the lockers. He told me to wait for him with Mom and Dad. But when he came out to the car, the glove was nowhere in sight. "It's all messed up," my brother said, as if that was a reasonable excuse.

"What do you mean, 'messed up?'" I asked him. "Gloves are supposed to be messed up. They're not exactly Sunday School shoes!" I was plenty burned up by this time, and feeling pretty sure there was more to his not giving me his mitt than I could figure out. And a lot more than a cramp that had gone wrong in the pool. "What's going on, Bennett?"

Bennett offered me a stick of gum, and told me I'd get the glove by the end of the week and to please shut up. Couldn't I see he was under very high stress?

That night we went out for chili-burgers and Dad asked Bennett how his leg was feeling and suggested that maybe a doctor should look at it. Bennett said it was better, fine, in fact, and he didn't need to see a doctor. Mom must have had a talk with him because Dad then told Bennett that he wasn't going to pressure him to keep swimming for the team, but hoped Bennett would reconsider. While we were waiting for our order, Dad remembered something. "Did you see the kid with the painted toenails? They allow that?"

Mom said, "The girls are allowed, why not the boys?"

"Real boys don't wear nail polish, that's why," Dad answered, and I guess no one was in the mood to argue with him.

When he bought us each an ice cream sundae for dessert, he said that he hoped Bennett would "think hard" about not leaving the swim team.

Mom was very quiet. I guessed she was thinking what I was thinking: my brother had made a statement.

No one was going to force him to do anything.

"I hate the swim team," Bennett finally said. "I hate the school too. And you know?" He was holding his spoon in the air like a flag. "I guess I know how your father felt when he packed up and went to Argentina!"

6

For a few days after the meet, our house seemed eerie, like a virtual, not quite real home. I mean, we were doing our usual stuff, but nobody was acting like their actual selves. Bennett wasn't talking about the swim team and neither was Dad, Mom was misplacing her car keys but Dad was not even noticing, and I was not bugging Bennett about the glove. It was as if we were all on careful behavior, like somebody had just died.

I practiced my saxophone every day, and Dad asked Bennett to paint the lamppost in front of the house. Dad hardly asks about Bennett's schoolwork, because it's usually in the A category even though it seems to me he spends all his spare time playing video games, but I guessed painting stuff like the lamppost was a wholesome experience to substitute for swimming.

So, about a week later, Nolan and I were shooting baskets in the driveway, and Bennett was up on a ladder, painting. We could hear the commotion next door; as usual, there were a lot of kids hanging out at Terry's. Nolan and I were about to go inside for refreshments when Nolan stopped dribbling the basketball and said he thought he heard his brother's voice coming from next door. Sure enough, we walked around the hedge that separates our driveways and found his brother Jeremy walking around on stilts and showing everybody a kite he'd made out of old magazines. It looked kind of lop-sided, weird, and interesting, and so did he.

Nolan got him to hop off the stilts long enough to come over to our place, where I introduced him to Bennett.

"I heard about what happened at the swim meet," Jeremy said, back up on his stilts, and I didn't think that was the best way to begin a conversation with my brother, but then he said, "I was so slow at my old school track meet the kids called me 'Turtle Lightning'," and Bennett stopped painting, looked at Jeremy, and began to exhibit a little interest.

"Will that kite fly?" he asked Jeremy. Jeremy had tied the kite to one of his stilts, and was wobbling up there on them on the front walk, so he and Bennett, who was still up on a ladder, were almost at about the same eye level. When Jeremy finally hopped off the stilts, though, I could see he was really short for his age, about my height. And he was kind of bulky; you just knew he'd be the last kid picked not only for a track meet but also for any team whatsoever.

"It'll fly, but not that high." Jeremy untangled it from the stilt and watched Bennett paint for a few minutes, walking around the lamppost and telling him where he had missed spots.

Bennett climbed down the ladder to take a closer look at the kite, and I guess if you know a person as well as I know my brother, you could tell that some sort of light had sparked inside his head. I hadn't seen a look on his face like that in a long time.

"You made it yourself?" he asked Jeremy.

"Sure," Jeremy said.

"No kidding. How'd you do that?" he asked.

"Oh, I've made a whole bunch. Want one?"

"Sure," Bennett said, and that's how their friendship began.

Mom was inside soaking her feet, but when Bennett took Jeremy upstairs to show him his dog and cat stamp collection, the pictures of Frankie, and a few of his videos, she called upstairs. "Would your friend like to stay for dinner?" she asked.

I thought calling Jeremy "your friend" was not exactly on the money at that point, but she must have definitely felt something in the air because she added, "We're having ravioli." That is the house special, food Dad calls "the magnet meal," because my friends always ask to stay over if it's on the menu.

Jeremy said, "I'll call home and ask my mother," and then very politely thanked Mom, which I could see created a jumbo impression. Mom was now in her slippers, looking into the refrigerator, and she was smiling at a jar of olives.

It turned out that Nolan stayed too, and that dinner completely restored the family to its real self. As soon as it was over, Dad complained about his shoulder, asked if I'd practiced the saxophone, and congratulated Bennett on a good painting job while Mom started dashing around looking for the box of coffee filters she swore she'd left on the top of the refrigerator.

As soon as Jeremy and Nolan left, Dad asked where the DeWitt family lived, used to live, how many of them there were, and a lot of questions he's never asked about any of *my* friends' families. Then he told Bennett he was happy to see that Jeremy seemed "pretty regular" and that flying kites seemed a very constructive and interesting hobby. I thought having a friend who was a triplet was more interesting than having a friend who made kites out of old magazines, but I knew not to say anything.

Mom said Jeremy had nice features and would probably grow out of his "stubbiness," and she commented on his table manners, which she graded as tip-top. "Did you see how he pulled the chair out for me?" she asked Dad, and had my father noticed how he wiped his mouth after every bite?

I thought Jeremy was maybe overdoing things, but my mother called him "a real gentleman," and said she hoped Bennett would be seeing more of him, and she and Dad exchanged meaningful, parent-type looks.

"A nice boy," Dad said, and got up to help Mom find the coffee filters.

7

Things were back to normal at our house, but for me, there were going to be no happy endings until I got hold of Bennett's glove. My own outfielder's one was too small and a piece of the back web was torn. Meantime, I kept having to borrow other kids' mitts whenever there was a softball game. I started shadowing my brother at school whenever I could, trying to get him to open his gym locker to give me his, which seemed like a very simple thing that would take just about two minutes.

The problem was, our schedules were different, but there was more to it. He always tried to duck me, was too busy, or said he was too involved with other "high priority" stuff. "Will you get off my back, Matthew?" he said a lot. I don't know how long it took me to figure out that for some mysterious reason he didn't want me to get anywhere near that glove. It took me an even longer time to get the bell ringer that this had something to do with him crying in the middle of the night.

But now Bennett had someone to sit with in the school cafeteria. He and Jeremy were getting real tight, and whenever I went by their table, there was this boring conversation about kites that I was not supposed to interrupt. It was another way for Bennett to get out of doing what I wanted him to do. On the other hand, he must have felt guilty, because a lot of the time he handed me extra cookies he'd managed to smuggle into his lunch bag from the highest kitchen shelf, where Mom keeps thinking they're out of reach. He also gave me the amazing baseball feats video he got for his birthday a couple of years ago.

When it got to be Thursday, Bennett and I had a big fight at breakfast. Last weekend it had rained Saturday and my team softball practice had been canceled, but today the TV forecast for the weekend was sun, and I was still without a decent glove to call my own. Dad was in Toledo and Mom was looking for the nail polish remover she'd been searching for for a week, so neither of my parents were around when my brother and I got into a breakfast rumble right between our orange juice and scrambled eggs. I don't know who started it, but all of a sudden there were pieces of toast and balled up napkins whizzing back and forth and Bennett still wouldn't tell me when exactly, at what moment, he'd open his locker and hand over the mitt.

"Just give me the combination!" I yelled, not for the first time, and that was another weird thing about my brother. He said he'd rather clean school toilets than let any living person know the combination of his lock. You would have thought he was a diamond smuggler instead of an eighth-grade kid with old shorts and T-shirts, a couple of towels and his catcher's mitt stashed away in a school locker. Of course I thought drugs right away, but I know Bennett and he's very thumbs-down on C and H and E, anything that starts with any letter of the alphabet that gets kids high. He said he once saw a guy so zonked and near death in the boys' room he was scared off for life.

Mom had to leave before she'd found her nail polish remover and told us to "stop-fighting-right-this-minute!" and act our ages. "If this mess isn't cleaned up in five minutes—" she said, and that's when we ran out of the house so we wouldn't be late for the bus, promising to get the place in shipshape the minute we got home from school.

A quieter version of the fight continued on the school bus. I thought I'd finally won the round when Bennett promised to meet me at the lockers at the beginning of lunch period and hand over the mitt. I told him if he didn't show up I would squeal to Dad and he would probably slap a wall and maybe make Bennett paint the house top to bottom. "So, don't forget!" I warned him.

"Okay, okay, I hear you," Bennett said.

As I was about to fly out the door of my Social Studies class, which is my last period before lunch, Mr. Manheim returned my global studies report. I am bad at Math but good at Social Studies, and got an A minus. Mr. Manheim held me up, wanting to explain the minus, which was because the Power Point pie chart graph wasn't perfect. He didn't take that long, but I guess I was delayed by about five paragraphs; Mr. Manheim does not talk in simple sentences. Even so, I was feeling pretty good when I sped to the locker room at breakneck speed. I admit I got there late, like five minutes after the bell, but Bennett wasn't at his locker or anywhere nearby, for that matter. I watched the second hand on the clock over the door go round and round as the minutes ticked by. Now the minute hand was moving too, and of course I waited, and *waited.*

It was seven minutes past, then eight, then ten. When I looked up at the clock again, it seemed to be turning colors, which meant I was getting really bummed just looking up there, watching time march on. I figured Bennett must have been here, stayed ten seconds, then took off. I wasn't only mad, either. Now I was hungry as anything, and considered sitting right here and eating my chicken salad sandwich on the grungy bench between the lockers, in case he came back. But Nolan was waiting for me and so were a few of the guys I play ball with, so at a quarter past, I cut loose and headed for the cafeteria.

No problem finding my brother. Bennett was in his usual spot with Jeremy, finishing *his* chicken salad sandwich and reaching for one of his peanut butter cookies. Before I could say a word, he said, "Where were you, Matthew? I was at the locker one minute after the bell, but you weren't there!"

In a way, knowing what I know now, I think I should have let it all go. "You couldn't wait like three minutes, Bennett?" My voice was pretty turned up and I saw the cashier look our way. So did some kids at the tables next to my brother's, and Jeremy stopped eating one of my brother's peanut butter cookies, probably waiting for more excitement. It came pretty fast; I grabbed my brother's notebook and stepped back a foot. "You get this when I get the glove!" I said, holding it over my head, and before he could leap out of his chair to grab it, I took off like a shot through the lunchroom.

There was quite a chase, with me snaking between

tables, not hard because I'm smaller than my brother, and Bennett yelling, "I need that notebook next period, Matthew!" and never catching up. I went out the lunchroom door, cut a quick left and made for the stairs. I hid in a cubicle in the boys' room on the second floor for a minute, where there was nothing to do except examine Bennett's notebook, which used to be covered with decals of old-fashioned soda pop bottles and now had a bunch of kites drawn all over it. When I thought Bennett had lost the scent, I headed for my homeroom. There I stashed the notebook in my desk and then, dog hungry by this time, I took a right turn, the quickest way to the cafeteria, to eat my lunch.

But Bennett had figured me out. No one ever said my brother wasn't smart. I wasn't ten steps away from homeroom when he found me, about to run down the stairs. He got me by the arm and said he'd twist my left hand off this very minute if I didn't give him his notebook, which if he didn't have it next period, would get him into serious jelly.

I stood my ground, we tangled a couple of minutes until Mrs. Duncan, the music teacher, stopped us, pulled us apart, and gave us a lecture and got us to shake hands. Then, I really won. I went to get Bennett's notebook and together, we headed for the locker room.

8

I suppose one of the things that will stick in my head for the rest of my life is the way my brother's face looked when he opened his locker and pulled out the paper bag that had the glove in it. He looked as if he'd stepped into quicksand. When the door to the locker squeaked open, I got to look inside and right back there next to his gym shorts and balled up socks I spotted something else that spooked me.

"What are you doing with Mom's nail polish remover?" I asked my brother as he handed me the paper bag, but as soon as I pulled the mitt out, I began to get the big picture.

The glove was a yucky mess. It looked as if Bennett had used the nail polish remover to try to erase what somebody had written all over it, but when that didn't work, he'd rubbed off some parts of the leather. The mitt looked like something you'd see sticking out of a trash bin waiting for a garbage pickup. "Who messed up your glove like that?" I asked, but although I had a pretty good idea, I could see it wasn't going to be easy to get a definite answer. "I told you it was cruddy, didn't I?" my brother said.

"Not like this! And it smells like a manicure too!"

"Where's my notebook?" was my brother's answer. "Come on, Matthew, where'd you stash my notebook?"

"It's dis-gus-ting!" The thoughts of why anybody

would wreck my brother's expensive mitt were not at the moment my first order of business. It goes without saying the condition of the glove was a heavy letdown and I felt fizzled out. How was I going to play with this destroyed piece of leather? "Was it Go-go?" I knew Shearon would never do anything like this and my brother's no-answer answer made it pretty clear.

"Why did he do it?" I kept asking as my brother followed me up to my homeroom. "Why, Bennett? Why?"

As soon as I handed him his notebook, my brother finally got some words to come out of his mouth. He grabbed hold of my shoulders and looked down hard at me. "Don't tell Mom or Dad about this, Matthew, okay?"

Even though we threaten a lot, Bennett never rats on me and after I got past kindergarten age I've never told on him. I could have reminded my brother of that, but instead I just stood there with the glove in my hand wondering if I could put it through the washing machine or send it to the dry cleaner's. "Are you going to get back at Go-go for doing this?" I asked Bennett as he was walking out the door.

"Are you kidding?" Bennett said. "Have you lost it, Matthew? Ever hear anybody getting back at Go-go?"

"He won't get away with it!" I said, but of course, it was wishful thinking. People like Go-go get away with everything. Then again, I thought of the picture of the blindfolded lady with the scales that hangs on a wall in the auditorium. That's Justice. Looking at the mucked-up mitt in my hand, I thought sooner or later she might just come through.

Bennett thought that if we soaked the mitt in dishwasher detergent for a day or two, maybe we could clean up all the black smudginess and the few roughed-up places wouldn't really matter on the field. I had my doubts, but while Bennett was running water in the bathroom sink, Dad came home. Mom was working so he'd brought in some chicken takeout and after we finished, Dad told me to go to the basement and begin saxophone practice. I'd mastered the Sousa march and had a new piece to learn, "We Are the World." The school band would be playing both at Bennett's graduation in June. I would have to know "the entire repertoire" perfectly, Dad kept reminding me.

In the meantime, while Bennett and Dad were cleaning up the kitchen, I heard their voices and enough of the conversation to know my father was giving Bennett a late-model We Must Strive talk. Even after the disaster of the swim meet, I could tell Dad was trying to get some kind of a commitment from my brother, probably trying to interest him in some other team. Soccer, I would bet. Dad used to play it; even though he likes golf now, he still has shin guards and a shirt he wore with his team name on it. Dad's ideas seem fixed in his head with iron glue, but luckily he let me off the soccer hook when I started playing softball. Now he was saying he didn't want Bennett just hanging around after school, doing nothing and getting into trouble in his teenage years.

I stopped playing long enough to hear Bennett offer to cook dinner when Mom had to work evenings. I heard Dad laugh and guessed he thought that was pretty funny, but I knew Bennett wasn't kidding. Believe it or not, he really likes watching the Food Channel on TV, and he once cooked a hot chili that was hot in every sense of the word.

That was the last of my eavesdropping. I had to make music or Dad would run downstairs to see why I wasn't blowing my notes, but I wasn't down in the basement more than fifteen minutes when he called down to me from the top of the stairs. "Matthew, Matthew!" His voice sounded urgent. "Come upstairs!"

I put down my saxophone, expecting trouble. Of course, I was thinking he'd discovered the glove in the bathroom sink.

But it had nothing to do with the glove.

"Come and look at this!"

When I got to the kitchen, there they were, Dad and Bennett, the evening newspaper spread out across the table. "Isn't this the guy?" Dad asked me, pointing to the picture of a face I knew I'd seen before.

"Bennett was under water and isn't sure, but you and I saw this kid, didn't we? Wasn't he racing against Bennett, right in the next lane at the swim meet?"

I looked at the face in the photograph. It took me a minute, but I recognized him although he looked like a younger version of himself; it was the kid from Whitney Young Junior High. The one with the painted toenails.

The headline over his picture made me jump, really jump:

EAST HADLEY YOUTH VICTIM OF HATE CRIME

"A bat-and-rope-wielding gang attacked Kevin Delaney, a student at Whitney Young Junior High

School, as he was rollerblading in a Jefferson park last night. Delaney's father told police that a group of approximately five youths surrounded him, taunting him with homophobic epithets. Two of the youths clubbed the victim and one produced a rope, putting Delaney's head through the noose. A passerby summoned the police and the crowd dispersed at the sound of the police car siren. It was not the first gay-bashing incident in this city; last year similar incidents were reported in and around the area. Police are asking for anyone with information about this attack to come forward."

I didn't understand some of the words in the article. "What does homophobic mean?" I asked Dad.

He corrected my pronunciation and said, "It means having an aversion to gay people."

So then I asked, "What does 'aversion' mean?" I know gay men are the ones who fall in love with other men. Gay women are like Gretchen and Valerie, the two ladies who live on the corner of our block and have a big white cockatoo that can talk, named Blanche. I sometimes do errands and stuff for them.

"Aversion means 'dislike'," Dad said. All this time, Bennett was staring down at the paper without saying a word. I never knew him to take that long to read anything.

"It's terrible, the way some kids behave," Dad went on, shaking his head. "Hoodlums, those boys. I hope they don't get away with this! That poor boy must have been scared out of his wits."

"Why do they dislike gay people?" I asked, and Dad just shrugged and said, "No good reason." Then he looked up at the kitchen clock and said it was getting late. "Are you through reading that, Bennett?" When Bennett said he guessed so, Dad picked up the newspaper and turned the pages, looking for the sports section, his favorite. When he found it, he folded the paper into quarters and headed for the living room.

My brother was about to take out the trash when Dad stopped in the doorway. "But I'll tell you one thing, boys. I spotted that kid in the water right away, didn't I? Painted toenails! I knew there was something funny about him right away."

9

When I got up the next morning and checked on the glove, it looked worse than it had the night before. I stuck it on the bathroom windowsill to dry and hoped that by the time I got home there would be some improvement. All day in school I kept my eyes open for Go-go too. I wanted to ask him face to face why he'd done what he did, after my brother was nice enough to lend him his mitt and give him brownies. But Go-go wasn't in the cafeteria at lunch; some of the kids said he was in detention, some said he'd sneaked out for a hot dog, but I finally saw him in the school lobby at the end of fifth period. Last year the principal set up a ping pong table there just like the one in our basement, and that's where he was, red-in-the-face, trying to beat the school ping pong champ.

"Why'd you do it?" I asked Go-go. "What made you take my brother's glove—"

"Can't you see I'm in a competition here?" Go-go cut me off. He was annoyed, but so what.

"You can answer one question! Why did you mess up Bennett's glove? My dad gave him that mitt and it was almost new!"

Go-go missed a shot, the ping pong ball flew off the table and bounced on the floor in my direction. I picked it up and handed it back to him. "Just tell me!" I said.

"Will you get lost! Fade out, Matthew!" Go-go said. "I just lost a point, thanks to you, twerp!"

"TELL ME!"

Go-go lifted the paddle like he was going to whap me with it just as the bell rang. I guess for people like Go-go being late for class doesn't mean much, but for me, even if I walk in only two minutes after the bell, it's blue ruin. Especially to Mr. Gold's Math class, where I was heading now.

"I'll tell you one of these days, but you won't want to hear it. Your brother's a *freak*! A *pervert*!" Go-go called after me as I started running to class.

"He is not, is NOT!" I yelled back. "*You're* the freak!"

I wished a big fist would come out of the sky and just smush him like an ant; I told myself one day it would. Nobody deserved it more.

I stayed after school for band practice, and when I got home, I ran right upstairs to examine the glove. It was still soppy and looked worse than ever. The situation was hopeless. Mom was in the kitchen and the first thing I noticed were her fingernails, which looked okay. I guessed she'd given up and bought another bottle of polish remover. She was doing a crossword puzzle and looked cheerful too. "Your brother is in the basement with his new friend," she said. I could see what was left of the banana bread she'd served them, and sat down with her to have a chunk before it disappeared, like the brownies.

"He seems like a nice boy, don't you think so?" she asked. I said I thought so.

"His brother is great," I reminded her. Nolan was home doing chores but would be over tomorrow afternoon. Mom asked more questions about the family. "His father is a big executive in a company and they get free soap and shampoo all the time," I told her. Mom gave me a hug. "Isn't that nice?" she said. "Maybe we'll invite his parents over for dinner one night."

After I finished two pieces of banana bread, I went down to the basement to discuss the mitt with my brother. I never told him what Go-go had called him; I'd tried to put it completely out of my head. I think what I wanted for Bennett to do was to make Go-go pay for a new one, although down deep I knew wishing for a trip through the galaxy to check out new planets would have been easier. Jeremy and my brother were standing over our ping pong table, the net was down, and Jeremy's kite stuff was all over the place. "We got a new white pet rat. His name is Felix," he said. "He's very cute and we're going to teach him tricks. Dad brought him home from the company lab and saved him from experiments."

I didn't want to talk about the DeWitts' pet rat. I wanted to know what Bennett was going to do to get me a good catcher's glove by Saturday.

"At the moment, Jeremy is teaching me how to make a kite," Bennett said when I brought up the subject. He assured me we'd talk about it later. I wanted to know how much later. "After dinner," Bennett said. I reminded him I'd be practicing "We Are the World" and then having Mom help me with polynomials. We just started algebra this year and I'm not getting the gist. Of course, no one else is either, except Kim Yee, the math star, so I don't feel all that bad. Bennett was squirting glue on some colored paper and stopped listening to me. "Later," he said.

"You can buy a new glove cheap on the Internet," Jeremy offered. It was easy; his father was ordering rat food that way.

"Where am I going to get the money?" I wanted to know.

"You can earn it." Bennett had once had a paper route but stopped because Dad didn't think delivering papers was a wholesome experience. He was worried when Bennett had to go through bad neighborhoods while it was still dark.

"Doing what kind of work?"

"Raking leaves," Jeremy suggested.

"It's April! They won't fall until September."

"Cutting grass, then."

"There's no grass growing yet. It's still too cold," I reminded him.

"You'll think of something."

Bennett held up a kite. "Look at this, Matthew. All it needs is a tail. Cool, isn't it?"

10

That night, Bennett showed Dad and Mom the kite he'd created. It looked a lot like the ones Jeremy makes, but Mom and Dad admired it so much you would have thought he'd built a 747 instead of pasted together a bunch of old magazine papers. Bennett said he and Jeremy were going to bike down to Edgewater Point tomorrow after school and get their kites up and flying. "A nice sport," Mom said, rubbing Dad's sore shoulder. He said Jeremy's stilts were putting holes in the lawn, but he agreed.

Nolan, his brothers and I tagged along with my brother and Jeremy, and we biked down to the beach where for a while we watched them trying to get their kites to go up, up, and away. The whole thing looked pretty boring until the kites began to take off. Jeremy kept saying there was not enough wind, but after a few minutes, my brother ran to the edge of the water with his kite and the kooky thing actually began to climb. It was something to see; the way one minute it was a bunch of paper and sticks dragging along on the back of his bike and the next it was going up and staying in the sky like a new colored constellation. I guess I said "Wow" so loud that my brother turned to look at me, and I could see the "Wow" written on his face too.

“It really is cool!” I told him, and then I asked Jeremy if he’d teach me to make a kite too.

“ASAP,” Jeremy promised.

Actually, it wasn’t until a few days later that Jeremy came by again. He had to wait for his allowance to come due so he could buy hardwood spools and graphite tubing, more glue and some spar ferrules, which connect skinnies to the tubing. It was a lot to buy, and a lot for me to learn. Jeremy was also washing his Dad and Mom’s car to make extra money, which all went for equipment needed even to make an ordinary diamond kite, no bigger than the flag flying in front of our school.

Finally, there it was, all this stuff we had to have spread out on our basement ping pong table, or so we thought. Halfway through, Jeremy told me to get some old magazines. He’d brought spools and string, even a couple of ribbons for the kites’ fancy tails, but he’d forgotten to bring the magazines. I went upstairs and asked Mom if she had any old issues of *Money Monthly* or *Medicine Today*, which are the two magazines that seem always to be lying around. She saves *Medicine Today* and didn’t want to give me any of those, and *Money Monthly* is pretty drab. I thought it wouldn’t look like much on the end of a string in the sky and anyway, she wasn’t sure Dad had finished reading through all the issues.

I suddenly remembered that Bennett had some magazines. That is, he had stashed some *Video Update* and *Small Screen Horror* issues somewhere in his closet, probably out of Mom and Dad’s (and my) reach. My parents prefer us to be into stuff that has ancient maps or dead presidents on the covers, reading materials teachers would assign and you'd hide comic books behind in Study Hall.

My comics are all over the place, but Bennett's stuff is stashed in boxes under other boxes back in the dark corners of his closet somewhere. I started to dig, and actually found a package of rock mineral samples I'd been missing for about a year and Bennett's old Boy Scout Camp photo album, gone for about two years, and of course his Christmas box of dog and cat stamps, but no magazines. It's not that Bennett is that neat, but sometimes he does tidy things, like putting wooden shoe forms in his shoes without being told, and folding his sweaters just like Dad does. This looked like one of those times, because I saw a yellow box at the very back of his closet that was tied around with like twenty rubber bands. I began pulling it out of the closet when I heard my name and footsteps running upstairs.

My brother burst into our room and bounded, really *pounced* through the door, as if he'd actually pole-vaulted in from the hall. He yelled "Matthew!" looking at the box in my hands as if there were explosives inside, ready to combust. "Matthew! What do you think you're *doing*?" he asked.

"Looking for a stash of nuclear warheads," I said.

Now my brother lunged at the yellow box and grabbed it out of my hand as if there really were nuclear-type weapons in there and we'd all be blown to smithereens in a minute.

I guess my mouth was hanging open with surprise as I watched my brother take the box under one arm and dig back there in his closet. He pulled out a broken umbrella, a box of keys to nowhere, two dented canteens, some torn shirts and a pair of rubber flippers. Finally he found what he was looking for: an old army blanket we used to keep at the back of Dad's car to use for picnics. Bennett wrapped the box in the blanket, told me not to touch it, go near it, to STAY OUT of his closet, and put it back in the farthest corner of the back, behind his rain slicker hanging on a hook.

Then he turned around and looked hard at me. I guess he already knew I wasn't going to let any opportunity go by. It's my nature to snoop; I can't help it. It's like the color of my eyes, locked into me for life. As soon as I figured when Bennett would be out of the house, I'd dig out the yellow box. Maybe whatever was in it would help me get a handle on what was really going on with my older brother.

11

We finally found some very old magazines in the attic and worked all afternoon finishing our kites. Bennett would have run right out to fly his the minute he'd glued on a tail, but it was drizzling and there were thunderstorms expected. "Dangerous!" Jeremy knew of a kid in his old neighborhood hit by lightning holding a kite, so although it wasn't raining that hard, we didn't go out that day. It was the next afternoon that we headed to the park, when the sun was beaming, the wind was blowing just enough to make the school flag fly and leaves in the trees flutter. In other words, weather conditions were perfect.

The park, it turned out, was not the best place for kite flying, and that afternoon finished kites for me, probably for the rest of my life.

We got there on our bikes around four and began preparing our lines, getting ready to get last minute instructions from Jeremy. The first instruction was never to call the line "string." "It's uncool," he said. There were kids throwing Frisbees in the big open meadow so we had to move to another section of the park to a smaller field, the one nearer Knickerbocker Avenue.

I was pretty wired up when we first started. I imagined this first flight as just the beginning, and soon I'd be building bigger kites, box kites, kites the size of helicopters. I actually imagined myself lifted off the ground, flying over the trees, creating a paper pterodactyl that would carry me through the air on a jet stream. I think I was catching Bennett's excitement and obviously getting completely carried away.

"Stand with your back into the wind and hold your kite up as high as you can," Jeremy instructed us. Bennett stood a few feet away from me and we did exactly what Jeremy told us to do. "Now don't get excited and throw it into the air!" he told us as I began getting excited and throwing it into the air.

"Not too much line or it's going to start spinning out of control," he went on. All this time, he was getting his kite to slowly float up, while Bennett's and mine were still kind of dragging across the grass. I noticed there were a couple of people standing around watching, and as Jeremy's kite began climbing, more people gathered. At first I was kind of embarrassed, but now, all of a sudden, I felt a tug on the line I'd wound around my hand, the wind picked up my own kite, and like I'd performed a magic trick, it began to float up. A few people cheered. Someone whistled. I'll admit it was a really nice feeling, even though the line began cutting into my fingers. I was thinking I'd have to invest in a spool, but in the meantime, I was watching my kite go up over my head, head towards the sky, and climb higher and higher. I heard my brother yell, "Hey, Matthew, wow! GO!"

"Watch out for that tree!" Jeremy was busy keeping his eye on his own kite and mine too. Bennett's kite was still bouncing around near the ground. To tell the truth, it felt pretty good to beat out my older brother, but now I was worried, because my kite looked as if it was veering off toward the high branch of a big tree up ahead.

"Pull in the line a little!" Jeremy called out to me. His own kite was sailing straight up, looked like it was aiming right for the lowest cloud, which seemed to be hanging right above us. "Make sure the nose is pointing straight up, Matthew!"

Now Bennett's kite began climbing too. He was not far from me, talking to it. "Finally woke up from a snooze!" He sounded really happy. "Get up there! Go, go, go, kite! Get up there!"

I was watching my kite, green tail, and Bennett's too, red-and-white tail, and both kites were up there now, really levitating along nicely, getting smaller and smaller in the sky. Bennett's went left, mine went right, and Jeremy's was so high we almost lost sight of it.

Then someone in the crowd yelled out. "Watch out! Watch out! That kid's kite is gonna hit the power line!"

I didn't know they were talking about me. I had no time to think, or to act, and for a minute, I didn't know what hit me. What blindsided me was not a jolt of electric power, it was my brother, who tackled me, pulled down my kite, and sent me smashing into the ground.

"You almost got electrocuted!" he was gasping. I was too shook to realize he might have saved my life. The line felt like it was cutting my fingers in two, and since I'd fallen down hard on my knees, they felt as if they'd been hit with hammers. For a second I couldn't catch my breath.

"One more inch and your kite would have hit that power line!" Bennett was panting and a few people in the crowd came running towards us, thinking maybe I'd been zapped from the wires after all. "You all right? Is he okay? Is he hurt?" people were asking. "He's okay," Bennett said, and pretty soon Jeremy was there helping me untangle the line from my fingers.

"I didn't see it! I'm new here!" he kept saying. He was looking down at me, very upset, and kept apologizing all over the place for not noticing the power lines right next to the row of trees at the edge of the park.

It wasn't until a few minutes later I noticed that Bennett's kite was now stuck up high in the limbs and leaves of one of them, and it looked twisted, definitely and completely ruined.

He was helping me up and really sweating. "Are you really okay?" he kept asking, and he got red around the eyes, like Dad does.

I didn't say it then and there, but right away, as I was brushing the grass and dirt off my shirt and rubbing my knees thinking maybe they were both broken in seven places, I decided I'd stick to softball. And the saxophone. Hitting a ball with a bat and making music seemed a lot safer way for me to spend my time.

12

Although I was turned off kites for life, my brother wasn't. Almost every day, Jeremy came pedaling down our driveway with all sorts of kite equipment strapped to the back of his bike. Together he and Bennett worked while the stereo blasted—mostly Nirvana. Jeremy's stilts were permanently stashed at our house and I tried them once or twice, but fell off every time. Down in the basement the kites were getting bigger and better; Jeremy had sent away for some plastic stuff and he and Bennett began painting swirls and stripes all over the new models. Now they said using cut-up old magazines was "kid stuff."

All this time, I was waiting for my opportunity to run upstairs and check out the yellow box at the back of Bennett's closet. As I said, I was born to spy and hadn't forgotten the stash for a minute. I figured the best time would be when my brother was not in the house. It might take time to go through the junk piled back behind Bennett's clothing and shoes and stuff, take out the mystery box, take off the blanket around it, and then put everything back in order again.

The problem was that when Bennett and Jeremy were at the park or at the beach trying out their new kites, I was out in the neighborhood looking for odd jobs. I wanted to earn enough money to buy my own leather mitt. The wrecked one was still lying around on the windowsill up in our room, and I wanted to smack a wall like Dad every time I looked at it.

So far, I'd made a few dollars washing cars. Once I did some errands for an older lady on our street, and once I fed Blanche the cockatoo when Valerie and Gretchen were away for the weekend. As Dad put it, so far I'd accumulated enough for about a thumb and a finger of the glove, but one night when he was in a very good mood, he said he'd match my funds, which put me in a very good mood too. It was the very next day that my opportunity to search through Bennett's closet came.

He and Jeremy's latest kite looked like a big yellow eagle with a black-and-yellow tail. All Bennett's allowances had gone for the dowel rods, paint, plastic, bamboo, glue, and I don't know what-all else that was cluttering up our ping pong table. This was their biggest project so far, and Bennett had painted dots and arrows on the eagle's wings to make it look like a bird from space instead of anything you'd see flying around in real life. It was big too, probably bigger than a real eagle, not that I've ever seen one. Dad said it was pretty impressive, and agreed to come down to the beach on Saturday for the lift-off.

I was invited too, but I had to carry stuff to the recycling center for Mom, pick up meds at the drug store for a sick neighbor down the street and clean out Blanche's cage. When I got home from doing all of it, I was pooped and ready for a little milk, cookies, and R and R, but I also discovered that I was all alone in the house. The family was still at the beach watching the kite launch.

You would have thought my feet were battery-operated the way I high-tailed it upstairs to Bennett's closet. I knew I'd have to do my investigation in a major hurry because who knew when they'd all come walking back into the house? On the other hand, it was still pretty early, and I figured after the beach Dad might take everyone out for a soda to celebrate. He and Mom were so happy with Bennett's new hobby and best friend, there were little soda and ice cream celebrations happening all the time. When Nolan came by, we'd get the usual doughnut holes or oatmeal cookies. For Bennett and Jeremy, when Mom was home, she'd go way over the top, pouring sprinkles on ice cream or concocting special smoothies in the blender. I told Nolan it was like Jeremy was a visiting prince. He and I were just commoners.

I began digging in the closet by being very careful to remember the order of things I had to take out to get to the blanket in the back. I didn't just dive in, the way I wanted to. I didn't stop when, of all unexpected things, I ran across a bag of glass marbles I hadn't seen since fourth grade, but just kept going, burrowing through stacks of this and that—until I stopped. Speaking of unexpected things, just as I heard Dad's car pull up, I had my hand on the blanket and pulled out the box.

The rubber bands were gone so it was easy to open, and my blood whizzed around in my head as I rushed to take a look.

Bennett must have guessed I'd dig until I got my hands on the box he wanted to hide. I should have known it; my brother knows my nature probably better than I do. And now I figured this was serious secret business or he wouldn't have gone to all the trouble of making sure I'd never be in on it.

The box was empty!

"You home, Matthew?" Dad's voice was calling. I barreled around like I was motorized, putting everything back in the right order, then went downstairs. There they all were in the living room, waiting to tell me about the plastic eagle that had flown almost a hundred yards into the sky above the beach. "You should have been there," Mom told me, and then as she headed to the kitchen, all smiles, to begin preparing dinner, she asked if Jeremy wanted to stay. "I'm making ravioli. What do you say, Jeremy?"

13

About two Saturdays later, I finally had enough money to buy the new glove! Mom was working, which left Dad to take me to the mall, but I told him we could order one from the Internet. I'd just come in from cleaning Blanche's cage and washing Valerie and Gretchen's SUV, and handed Dad the ten dollars they'd just paid me and all the other money I'd stashed away in the baseball-shaped bank I've kept my money in since second grade. Dad agreed I'd have about a thousand more choices of mitts at an Internet sports shopping site. "Go upstairs and turn on the computer and I'll be right up." He had to put away the groceries he'd just carried in from the car.

I suppose I was pretty excited and took the stairs two at a time. At first I'd wanted to go to a real store and take the glove home right then and there instead of waiting for it to be mailed to me, but Dad was sure it would arrive in time for the following Saturday's softball game. By the time I reached the top of the stairs, I realized Bennett was using the computer. The door to Dad's office was closed, but I heard music coming out of the speaker. It wasn't Nirvana, it wasn't loud, it was like drums and a synthesizer. I didn't knock although I'm supposed to, but as I said, I was pretty charged and hyper, my mind on only one thing: the kind of mitt I was going to order.

So I burst into Dad's office, ready to tell Bennett I'd

need the computer for a couple of minutes, but the second I stepped into the room, I froze. What I saw on the screen really stopped me cold.

"What are you looking at?" I asked my brother, and my voice squeaked like it was coming from a beak instead of a mouth. His eyes got those red rims and he swiveled back and forth in his chair, looking really spooked. He'd pushed the mouse to the x but not fast enough. "Bennett! What is that—?"

He cut me right off. "You're supposed to knock! Why didn't you knock?!"

"I thought—" I began, but didn't know how to finish the sentence. "I thought," I began again, but Bennett cut me off again.

"Anyway, I was only poking around. That just jumped up on the screen." He pointed to the monitor, which was now a blue-green blank. "Don't look so shocked, Matthew! Just a slipup, a goof. I pushed a couple of the wrong buttons—"

I know when my brother is alibiing.

For a minute I was speechless. I just stood there, letting it sink in. Then, although what I'd seen was still hanging in the air, I told him I needed to use the computer. "Dad and I are going to order my new mitt."

"Dad's home? I thought he was out at the supermarket." Bennett's eyes were still circled in red, reminding me not only of Dad, but also the way they looked when he'd climbed out of the water at the swim meet.

"He just got home," I told him.

"When?"

"A couple of minutes ago."

My brother took a minute to think about this. "Okay, Matthew. Don't blab to him about this, okay? Or anyone?"

I told him I'd never mention it; why would I? "Just a couple of naked men dancing. No big deal," I said.

"No big deal," Bennett said, and he got up from the computer, swiveled the chair in my direction, and headed for the basement. "Just forget about it, okay?"

"Just did," I assured him, but of course, there was no way I ever could.

The day I brought my new mitt to school, my brother and Jeremy were at their usual spot in the lunchroom. I admit I'd brought it to the cafeteria to show off to the triplets and a few of the guys. They were standing around admiring the oil-treated steerhide leather, the rawhide laces. Even Nolan, who is a lefty and couldn't use a right-handed mitt, was trying it on. All of a sudden Go-go Mallis appeared from nowhere. His antennas must have been up and he spotted the glove from his own corner of the cafeteria, where he always sits with a bunch of guys he calls his amigos.

Before I knew what was happening, he was next to me, asking if he could look at it for just one little second. Of course, I had no intention of letting him anywhere near it, so I backed away. "Come on," Go-go kept saying. "I'm not gonna hurt it, Matthew!"

"NO WAY!" I was walking backward, ready to run, if necessary, when one of the amigos came up behind me, grabbed the mitt out of my hand and tossed it over my head. Go-go caught it. He threw it back out of my reach again and he and his buddy went on like that for a very long minute, while I was yelling at them to give it back, RIGHT NOW.

Of course everyone in the whole cafeteria was watching us by this time, and before I knew what was happening, Bennett came streaking across the room, with Jeremy right behind him.

"Give my brother back his glove!" Bennett yelled at Go-go. Go-go ignored him completely and turned the glove back to his buddy.

"DID YOU HEAR ME, GO-GO?" My brother's voice sounded like the high notes on my saxophone. "GIVE IT BACK!"

Go-go's friend threw it back to Go-go and Go-go swung it so high in the air that it hit a light fixture and bounced off it, falling on someone's lunch. Chocolate milk spilled across the table, and that's when I grabbed the mitt back, wiping it down with a napkin quick as I could. I could feel I was getting hot all over; Go-go had almost wrecked *my* glove too!

"If you ever touch my brother's mitt again, I'll—" Bennett's hands were balled-up fists; a crowd had gathered. I wondered when a teacher was going to show up to break things up.

"You'll WHAT? Spank me with a feather?" Go-go has a laugh that makes you think of buzz saws.

I know my brother doesn't like fighting, but now he looked ready to go into the ring with any heavyweight in America. "You're BAD NEWS, Mallis, and you're gonna get yours!" Bennett was breathing very hard. He took a couple of steps toward Go-go.

"Oh yeah? Like from who? Not you, Auntie Bennett!

Everybody knows you're nothing but a fruit-market twinkie!"

The amigos burst into a big laugh at that. It echoed through my head long after Mr. Manheim appeared, ordering Go-go back to his table and telling everyone to simmer down instantly! I looked down at my new glove, the smooth brown leather, the gorgeous way the fingers were stitched and the laces looped, and the little stain from where the chocolate milk had splattered it. I sat there trying to finish what was left of my own lunch and wished I'd never thought it was a good idea to bring the mitt to school.

14

The weather got warmer, and Mom invited Jeremy's whole family for a barbecue. For once Nolan and his triplet brothers were all dressed alike. They had on navy blue shirts and khaki shorts; even their sneakers and socks were the same. Mom kept saying how they were adorable and Dad said it was amazing; he knew I could, but he'd never be able to tell them apart. Their dad was very friendly and brought a whole bunch of soap shaped like dinosaurs for us from his company, and their mom had baked an upside-down cake that looked right side up to me.

I'd never met Nolan's older sister and I was pretty impressed; she had dyed her hair blue and had a tattoo of a sailboat on one arm and a pony on the other. "My favorite sport and my favorite animal," she explained, and told us she was going to have her tongue pierced. When Jeremy said he was going to get a white rat tattooed on one arm and a kite on the other as soon as he was old enough, his father said, "Over my dead body! One free spirit in the family is enough!"

That led to the conversation about kites and was the first I'd heard of the BIG PLAN. My brother and Jeremy were intending to build a very large, aerodynamic one-of-a-kind kite and fly it over the school athletic field during graduation ceremonies. It would be the biggest, most unusual box kite ever seen in town, and maybe in the whole state. My brother said it would be groundbreaking and dramatic and Jeremy said he and Bennett would be celebrities, remembered at our school as big wheels forever. He also said that he'd grown an inch and a half since moving to town from Chicago. He thought it was because he'd been spending so much time at the beach flying kites, breathing in healthy sea air.

"He loves coming to your house," Jeremy's mother said, and added, "I'm so glad he and Bennett found each other."

"So am I," Mom said, "so am I."

That night, when they thought I was playing the saxophone, I listened to the conversation Mom and Dad were having about Nolan's parents. They thought I was in the basement because Jeremy had once brought over a tape recorder and taped me practicing the Sousa march and "We Are the World." The tape was to be used only in emergencies or major league situations, like if there was a show on TV I couldn't miss or a conversation I really had to hear, like the one my parents thought they were having privately right now. I usually sit on the fourth step from the top of the stairs, where no one can see me but I can hear almost every word. Although Bennett painted the railing at least two times, you can still see the tooth marks from where Frankie chewed the wood when he was a puppy.

"They seem like nice people," was the gist of the first couple of paragraphs I heard. There was some back and forth about the soap they'd brought and the upside-down cake, which we'd finished off right after dinner. Some things were hard to hear because Mom was clattering silverware and running water and doing I-don't-know-what-all to make noise in the kitchen. It was when Dad moved into the living room and Mom followed that I got the major twists. "That daughter of theirs!" my father was saying. "Such a pretty girl, but what an oddball!" I didn't hear the rest of that sentence, which left a lot to the imagination, none of it good. Dad is not an oddball fan.

From the tone of her voice, I wasn't sure Mom agreed. Then Dad said he thought Jeremy was a bit "off the beaten track" and asked if Mom thought so too. She said he was "an exceptional child," which I thought could mean anything from being a genius to being a card-carrying nerd. Dad said it this time: "Anyway, I'm glad he and Bennett became buddies. I was beginning to be worried about that boy of ours; a boy without a single friend; I was beginning to think something might really be wrong with him."

All this time, while I was all ears on the fourth step, I thought Bennett was down in the basement gluing and painting while my saxophone tape was doing its practice thing. I really owed Jeremy for that stroke of good thinking is what was on my mind when I realized my brother wasn't in the basement at all. He was right behind me, listening to every word, like me.

"I'm glad he and Bennett became buddies," was the next-to-last sentence I heard Dad utter clearly. The last sentence, "I was beginning to think something might really be wrong with him," was the last. I know Bennett had heard it same as I did, and of course it really registered with me. It got locked into my head and I couldn't stop thinking about it—because of course I'd known it all the time: Bennett is cool, the greatest, and he's my brother, but there's no getting away from it. All the kids in school seem to know it, and there really is something very, very irregular about him. Whatever it is, I can't see it, maybe because he's my brother, but I guess it's like a radar to everyone else.

As soon as Dad said his sentences, Bennett left the top of the stairs. He went into the bathroom and a minute later I heard water running. I thought I'd better go see if he was okay and then I guessed I better respect his privacy, which he's told me to do about a thousand times.

I wondered what Dad would say if he'd heard the names Go-go called him. Or what he'd think if he saw what I saw on the computer screen in his office. I was actually scared Dad would be so upset he'd do something horrible, something worse than slapping a wall . . . something like just taking off, going to South America, and never coming back.

15

While Jeremy and Bennett spent every waking minute after school in the basement of our house bent over the ping pong table, Nolan, his brothers, and I spent a lot of time at his house trying to teach Felix new tricks. So far we'd gotten him to run up and down Nolan's arm and sit in a coffee cup. Bennett, meanwhile, had washed cars Saturdays, cleaned basements, even helped Dad nail some shingles to the roof, and whatever he earned went into equipment that arrived in the United Parcel truck. A new box of something kite-related seemed to get to our house every other day.

One night at dinner, Bennett asked Mom if there was a sewing machine anywhere in the house. He remembered her using one when he was little.

"I stopped sewing long ago," Mom said, "and I gave the machine to the church to sell at a charity sale."

"Do we know anyone else who has one?" Bennett asked.

"What are you going to do with a sewing machine?" Dad wanted to know.

"We're using nylon ripcord and need to sew panels of different colors together," Bennett explained.

"You're going to take up sewing now? Instead of swimming or hockey or Little League?" Dad's voice had a good-natured little ha-ha to it, but it also had an edge.

I could tell he didn't really love the idea of Bennett working at a sewing machine. Not a wholesome experience, I guessed, but I wasn't sure exactly why.

"Well, what's wrong with that?" Mom jumped right in. "I think it's fine. All the best tailors have been men," she added very forcefully, and that added it up for me right there and then. Dad thought sewing machines were only for girls, which made it an open-and-shut case: he didn't want Bennett to do things only girls did.

"I'm only going to stitch together our kite," Bennett said. "It's not like I'm taking up sewing, Dad." He looked uneasy, kept putting his fork in and out of the mashed potatoes without actually scooping any up.

"You don't have to apologize for sewing, Bennett!" Mom said, glaring at Dad. "In fact, one of my patients has a sewing machine and I'm going to see if I can borrow it! Then I'll show you how to use it."

"Is the patient with a sewing machine a man, Lydia, or a woman?" Dad asked, raising one of his eyebrows. He had a little smile like he was making a point, but at the same time it was all a big joke. Mom was not amused.

"You're sending the boys the wrong messages," she said to him, and I felt a parental fight brewing.

"What's for dessert?" I broke in, trying to create a distraction. I hate it when Mom and Dad argue. I hate it when they ignore me too, which they did now.

But when Mom told Dad that Mrs. Dowd was a woman but for all she knew her husband had used the sewing machine every day of his life when he was alive, Dad backed off and Mom simmered down. "You're right, Lyd. Sorry, Bennett. I better get rid of some of my old-fashioned stereotypical ideas! I'm really pleased about your kite project. And if you need me to help at any time, I'm here, ready and willing!"

Bennett relaxed. He put a heap of mashed potatoes on his fork, pushed it into his mouth, swallowed, and burped one of his two-note burps. No one got really mad at him this time—"Not at the table, I've told you a thousand times, Bennett," Mom said mildly—and I was so relieved, I laughed out loud. Sometimes my brother uses that burp to relieve stress, I guess.

Pretty soon Dad got up and began to clear the table, and I assumed the subject was closed, but as he took away Bennett's plate, he began a sentence, "Although—" and there was this long pause, with all of us looking at him to see what would come next. Finally, he said, "It would be smart of you not to tell anyone at school that you've taken up sewing. It's really no one's business."

I looked at my brother's face and for once, it seemed like a flat-out blank I couldn't read at all.

It was about the same time the next day that I got a telephone call from Kim Yee, who wanted to find out which problems on page seventy-nine were the math homework assignment.

Mom took the call and passed the phone to me.

"Who is Kim Yee?" Dad wanted to know. We had finished dinner and I'd been stacking the dishwasher. Bennett was outside, carrying trash to the curb, and Mom was looking for a dessert recipe she'd cut out of the newspaper and misplaced. I covered the receiver when Mom said, "She's called Matthew at least three times this week," and gave Dad a big winky wink, while I could feel myself getting pink right down to my toes.

"She sits next to me in Algebra. She also sits next to me at band practice because she plays the saxophone too—the baritone version, and THAT'S ALL," I said, hoping I was making it clear that Kim and I were not going to become engaged any time soon.

"Is she cute?" Dad asked, and looked at Mom, while all this time I was moving out of the kitchen with the telephone, hoping Kim hadn't heard any of it.

"Adorable," I heard Mom say, "a heartbreaker-to-be."

"Ooolala," Dad said, and he and Mom were giggling, best friends again, unfortunately at my expense.

Kim said she'd written all her assignments down and left the information in her desk at school. I thought maybe she was something like Mom because the other two times she called were about the schedule for band practice she'd misplaced, and the pages we'd be covering for the exam in polynomials.

I told her to hold on while I went up to my desk and dug out the assignment.

I guess I must have some of my mother's genes because now it was me who couldn't find the green pad in which I write down all the school stuff. That's how I came to look behind and under things, practically tearing apart my room, looking for the pad, knowing Kim was waiting on the telephone. I guessed it must be somewhere here, could have fallen behind my desk or slipped between my bed and the wall, when I was writing on my stomach on my bedspread. I sometimes tuck stuff under the top bunk of my bed, too, and checked to see if I'd done that and forgotten I'd done it. Not there. But when I started moving things around, I saw something sticking out from under Bennett's mattress, something I'd never seen before.

I guessed then I'd found the stuff he'd taken out of the yellow box at the back of the closet, and it was WHAM, like I'd been hit with something, like I'd felt if the kite I'd flown in the park that day had really hit the power line while I was holding it. I stood there, I don't know how long, feeling I'd been electrocuted.

"Matthew!" Mom called upstairs. "Your friend is still waiting on the line! Are you coming down?"

For a minute, I couldn't find my voice. When I finally did, I told my mother to tell Kim I'd call her back. I knew I needed to be alone for a couple of minutes, to stop my head from buzzing and to think.

16

I found my green pad lying on the mouse pad in my Dad's office just where I'd left it before dinner. I guess I'd just absentmindedly dropped it next to the computer while I was emailing Grandma and Grandpa in Minnesota. Mom's parents expect me to let them know everything going on in the family because they say I can write better than anybody else under this roof. I don't think it's true, but buttering me up is their way of getting all the news. They're getting pretty old and peaky and I don't want to shake them up, so I only put in the sunshine and never—like tonight—the storms and the pitchforks.

I picked up the pad, then headed for the hall telephone, called Kim back and read her the assigned page numbers. We talked about band practice for a while and I thanked her for her offer to help me with polynomials on Saturday afternoon, explaining I couldn't come over because of softball. Finally, I went back upstairs to my room, lay on my bed, and stared at nothing for about a half hour. I suppose I was waiting for Bennett to come upstairs. Or maybe, I was wishing he wouldn't.

I wanted to ask him questions and I didn't. What had become spelled out and clear as cold water was something I think I knew all along, but just benched out of my head; I didn't really want to know.

I was actually half asleep when he came up. I hadn't

done one bit of homework, hadn't practiced "What the World Needs Now," had just vegged out on my bed, waiting. But as soon as Bennett came into the room, I'm not sure why, I jumped up and ran out. I felt something in my head zigzag in and out, back and forth, up and down. But first I went downstairs, took the telephone out of the kitchen, and stepped outside the back door with it. No one could possibly hear me on the back stoop. I dialed Nolan's number and his older sister answered. At first she sounded real disappointed it was me, and then she got very polite and asked about my family and sent regards to my parents and told me she'd really enjoyed meeting us all, blah, blah; all the time I was one big knot, shivering on the back steps, waiting until she decided to call Nolan to the phone.

He said he'd been teaching Felix more tricks when I called and now he was actually learning to answer to his name. "Listen," I said, my voice sounding like it was coming out of some other species, maybe mouse too, "I have a question. What exactly is a *pervert*?"

"It's someone who hangs out with Go-go Mallis!" Nolan said right away, and he laughed at his own wisecrack for about a whole minute.

When Go-go called my brother names, what stuck in my mind was "pervert," which is what people call people in school all the time. It's sort of a joke insult, like when someone says he actually likes the food they sell in the school cafeteria or thinks the vice principal would be someone you'd want to invite to your house for brunch. Now it had sunk in: I knew it meant more.

"No, I mean, the real meaning." I think I should have

put on a sweater before coming out. I was shivering, waiting while Nolan gave it thought. The dictionary was on Bennett's desk or I would have checked there first.

"I think it's somebody who does weird sex things," he finally said. "Why do you want to know?"

I wanted to tell him I thought that maybe my own brother was turning into one, but instead, I didn't answer for a minute, and then said, "Oh, I just heard it on TV," hoping he hadn't even heard me.

But he did. "What channel? What are you watching?" Nolan wanted to know.

"It's over. You missed it." I'm not a good liar, but what else was I going to say? At this point, my teeth were actually chattering.

I had another question. "What's a three-letter man, do you happen to know?"

"I don't know what it is here, but in Chicago, Illinois, it's another way of saying, 'fag'. A four-letter man is a 'homo.'"

That's exactly the moment the back door opened and Mom came out and asked me what I was doing out here in the cold and to come inside this minute, had I lost my mind?

Fag, fag, fag kept going through my head as I walked very slowly up the stairs to confront my brother, eyeball to eyeball.

He was sitting at his desk doing his homework, headphones on, and didn't look up when I came in. For a minute I just looked at the back of his head, thinking, *He doesn't look any different.* He doesn't look like a *fag* or a *homo* or a *pervert.* He looks like me, everyone says. Same nose. Mom's chin. Dad's eyes. You could see it even in photographs Mom has in old frames all over the house. To tell the truth, I can't even tell our baby pictures apart in the family picture album.

"Bennett," I said, but he hadn't heard me. I figured he was tuned into one of his Nirvana tapes, so I yelled, "Bennett!" This time he turned and took off the earphones.

He looked at me, a little annoyed. "What? I'm trying to study, Matthew."

"I found your dirty homo magazines, Bennett," I blurted out, and believe it or not, although I'm going to be thirteen in three months and two weeks and haven't cried since Mom caught my finger in the car door by accident when I was eleven, I burst into tears right there, turned on the waterworks, blubbered like an infant, and just couldn't stop.

17

How long I stood there, I'm not sure. Probably only a minute or two, but it seemed like I couldn't get myself calm for a big stretch of time. Bennett had jumped up from his desk, run to the door to make sure it was closed, then ran back to put his elbows on his desk and his hands up to cover his face. When he finally looked at me, not just his eyes but his whole head looked like he'd had heat stroke. It scared me so much I stopped crying and started hiccoughing; I thought I could have brought on some kind of blood fit. Bennett could faint or hemorrhage or something and it would be all my fault.

He just stared at me not saying anything, then got up and went into the bathroom, got me a glass of water, and watched me gulp it down. For a long time we just sat together in our room, both of us staring at the floor in a weird kind of not-knowing-what-to-say silence. I kept hoping he was going to come up with an excuse for having those magazines with big color pictures of men doing creepo things to each other, maybe would tell me they belonged to someone else. "Where'd you get them?" I asked him, hoping and wishing. He was still red in the face.

"A kid at Boy Scout Camp," he told me. "I don't even know why I kept them. I wanted to get rid of them but I was afraid to put them in the trash. I'm getting rid of them tomorrow."

I wasn't sure I believed that. He could have thrown them out if he'd really wanted to.

"You're really a pervert?" I finally got it out.

"I'm not a *pervert.* I think I'm gay," he said.

I tried to absorb what it meant. Was he going to fall in love with a guy instead of a girl? Wear dresses? Makeup? Talk in a high voice? "How did that happen to you?"

Bennett shrugged. "I don't know," he said. "I don't KNOW." He said he thought he was born that way. He told me I must never tell Mom and Dad. NEVER. "If Dad ever found out—" Bennett said, without finishing his sentence, and we both probably had the same horrific thought: If Dad found out, it would be a disaster. There was no telling what he'd do. He might really take off like his father had and just disappear forever.

"Can't you try to change yourself?" I asked my brother. "Get normal?"

"I've been trying all my life," Bennett said.

"Couldn't you get a girlfriend?" I suggested, thinking of Moira, but Moira had just been Bennett's buddy and then got a real boyfriend. Forget Moira.

My brother shook his head no like it weighed a hundred pounds.

"Does Jeremy know?" I asked, and he shook his head no again.

"But he'll find out sooner or later," he said. "Go-go is making sure the whole school knows. He wrote 'faggot' and 'queer' all over my mitt and was going to spray paint some more words on the door of my locker, but Mr. Manheim caught him. He's probably the one who got somebody on the swim team to leave Post-it notes stuck inside it."

"Post-its? What'd they say?"

Bennett wasn't going to tell me, but finally, he did. "'We don't need any queers putting AIDS in our pool.' Stuff like that. I guess I queered it all right. I lost our meet, didn't I?"

"You got a cramp!"

"In my head, not my leg!"

"You don't have AIDS?" I was horrified.

"Of course not!"

"Did they put notes in your locker when you were in Little League too?" I asked him.

"I found stuff in my sneakers. Not notes. Just toothpaste. And wads of chewing gum. And they called me names. Different words, same music. I never fit anywhere, Matthew, end of story. I'm a homo, I'm pretty sure, a square peg forever. Can't you see how everyone in school hates me?"

There was more Bennett told me later that night, when we were in bed and the lights were out. How he got "romantic feelings" for a member of the Stamp and Coin Club and wrote him a note that the kid showed everyone. Bennett dropped out because of it, and that's the night I heard him crying. That's how everyone in school knew too. He told me how someone tied a pink ribbon on his bike, how he felt whenever he was alone in the cafeteria—blackballed, shut out, a strange weed. "You don't know," he said, and it seemed like the words he was saying must have been back there in his head waiting to be let out maybe all his life. "You just can't ever know, Matthew. The times I feel twisted and dark and disgusting, how often I've prayed in church for God to come down and put a hand on me and make me like everyone else." He told me that when God didn't react, he turned to the moon. "At least I could see his face," Bennett said. I thought maybe it was a relief for him to find someone in the world he could spill things out to—besides Frankie. "Frankie knew," Bennett said then, and I think he was actually being serious. "A dog couldn't understand anything like that," I argued. I was all of a sudden feeling sort of like an older brother, not a younger one.

"Frankie wasn't just a *dog*," Bennett corrected, and I let it go. If you have no one in the world on your side, maybe he becomes much more than a dog to you.

I thought about not having even a single friend and everyone pointing fingers, calling you names, making fun of you. I imagined joining the swim team or stamp club or any other group of guys and becoming a moving, breathing, duck-soup target, fair game for everybody to take pot shots, cut you down, rip, pan, slam, and smear you. And all this was happening to my brother.

"You have Jeremy," I reminded him.

"Until he finds out," Bennett said.

"I won't tell, Bennett."

"You swear?" he was asking me.

"I swear."

"You'll never let even Nolan know?"

"I won't."

I hardly slept that night. I was torn up for Bennett, and

worried for me too. What if I was gay too, but didn't know it? We looked alike and had the same parents, all those matching genes, chromosomes, genomes. People said we even sounded alike. And I didn't have a girlfriend and didn't care about getting one, either. I thought about Kim Yee and Dad saying, "Ooolala," but I didn't feel *ooolala* about her, or about any girl at all.

Then I thought about what would happen if somehow Mom and Dad figured it out or got the word from someone in school. If Dad took off, what would happen to Mom and us? All the time I was awake, I thought Bennett was awake too. It was almost as if our lives had tipped over dangerously that night, and could never be set straight and put in order again.

18

A few days later, we all celebrated Dad's birthday. Mom made roast beef, Dad's favorite, and baked a cake that was the tallest and most lopsided chocolate cake she'd ever made. Bennett helped decorate it with candy balls that looked like golf balls, and Mom presented Dad with a new Number Five iron he'd use as soon as his shoulder felt better. Then, Mom being Mom, she couldn't locate the birthday candles. Bennett had a few sparklers left over from the Fourth of July, so he stuck those into the cake. I played "Happy Birthday" on my saxophone with only two small mistakes. I'd learned it last year in time for Mom's birthday and now it was tradition. Everyone applauded.

We all sang to Dad, and if you'd been walking by our house and looked into the windows of the dining room, you would have thought we were all one hundred percent upbeat, a real happy family. I kept thinking that it was lucky that no one could read my thoughts.

The best part of Dad's birthday was the gift that came from Grandma and Grandpa, the present he unwrapped last. They had sent him the coolest camcorder with an LCD color monitor and a digital zoom and a card that said he'd be needing it to record every minute of Bennett's graduation. They were hoping Grandma's bad knee wouldn't keep them from flying across the United States to see it.

Bennett and I had chipped in to buy Dad a pair of new sunglasses that went from light lenses in shade to dark lenses in sunlight, and after we were in bed, he came up to our room. We'd already turned off the lights, were both in bed, and he whispered, "Are you awake, boys?" I was going to pretend to be asleep because I thought we might be in for a We Must Strive talk but Bennett said, "I'm not asleep," and that's when Dad really fooled me. He stood there next to our bunks, said he loved us a lot and really appreciated the sunglasses. He told us that whenever anyone came to his office he showed off the pictures of us he had on his desk. Many of his friends had kids who'd gotten into trouble or were into drugs or both, but we were different; he was sure we'd never let him down. "I know I'll always be proud of you both," he said. Then he gave us each a kiss and said he'd been blessed at having two great sons who would surely grow up into fine and decent men.

As soon as he left, Bennett climbed down from his bunk and went to the window.

"What are you doing?" I asked him.

"I'm looking at the moon," he said.

"What for, Bennett?"

"Even though it's only a half moon tonight, I think there's a man up there, watching all of us."

He'd said that before. "You really think so?"

"Didn't you ever look up and see his face?"

The truth was, I did, but then again I thought the

moon's face was just a bunch of shadows or blotches that looked like eyes and a mouth. "Not exactly," I said.

"I never want Dad to find out about me."

I waited to see what that had to do with the moon. Bennett climbed back into bed. "The moon controls the tides, doesn't it? And the calendar? And the behavior of werewolves? Well, I think it has a power over all of us. When I look up in the sky during a full moon and see that face, I can see an expression clear as anything. He's not happy with me, Matthew. Dad thinks I'm decent, and I'm not. I'M NOT! The moon is on to me. I can see it in those blotchy eyes! They're glomming right down on me!"

Then, just as I was falling asleep, Bennett asked if I was still awake. "No," I said, and he told me he thought that if his rainbow kite flew high in the sky at graduation, he and Jeremy might make the front page of the newspaper. "Wouldn't that be cool?" he asked, but it was more a statement than a question.

I said, "Yeah, it would be."

"Dad would really be proud of me then," my brother said.

"Yeah, he would," I said, yawning.

"Then everything would be different," my brother said.

"Yeah, it would," I think I said before drifting off to sleep.

Mom brought home Mrs. Dowd's sewing machine that very week and you could hear the whirring hum coming from the basement every single day after school. First Bennett and Jeremy practiced on old rags Mom managed to find for them, and then they got serious. I sometimes watched them measuring and cutting pieces of colored stuff and sewing it together in stripes. Once in a while it would come out crooked and that would put Bennett in a bad mood because he had to throw away a lot of his mistakes. He said it was expensive, but this time the kite had to be absolutely perfect.

Every time I went into the basement the thing had gotten larger. I'd never seen a kite this big and I had my doubts they'd ever get anything this humongous to leave the ground. On the other hand, if blimps could float up in the sky, why not Bennett's kite?

He'd sent for seven nylon colors from the kite-supply place and put them in a certain order. He was guided by Mr. Gold, the Math and Science teacher, who explained a memory trick. If you thought of a rainbow as a boy named Roy G. Biv, the letters of that name would remind you of the colors of the spectrum: Red, Orange, Yellow, Green, Blue, Indigo and Violet—always in that order. Mr. Gold said that a rainbow is actually raindrops breaking up light into a color show and you can usually only see one when the sun is sinking. If you look for it you're likely to see it at the side of the sky opposite the sun. Usually it's best to find a rainbow during a sun shower, or right after a rainstorm, late in the afternoon.

I've never in my life seen a real one in the sky, and Bennett says they never look as bright as nylon in true life but an actual rainbow is something amazing. He said he saw one once when he was walking Frankie and would never forget it. From now on after a rainstorm, I knew I'd really keep my eyes open.

Mom was the cheerleader for the kite project. She was

also the supplier of doughnut holes, cheese and crackers, cold drinks and salted peanuts. One night I'd seen Bennett leave the house with a bundle under his arm and watched him turn the corner of our street. I knew he was getting rid of his stash of magazines and felt that maybe I could relax a little. Since I'd discovered his secret, life hadn't turned upside down as I expected; everything was still pretty normal. With the magazines gone, it didn't seem likely Dad would find out about my brother accidentally, the way I had. I tried to put all of it out of my mind.

The kite was getting more and more supercolossal, I was managing a passing grade in Algebra, and getting pretty good at "We Are the World." Mom was smiling a lot and Dad was wearing his new sunglasses and practicing using his new camcorder every chance he could. I wanted things to stay the way they were. Forever.

Dad videotaped us on our bikes, getting on the school bus, doing errands. He videotaped Nolan and me shooting baskets and Mom tossing a salad. He went next door and taped our new neighbor clipping his hedge and one day, he shot Bennett at Valerie and Gretchen's.

Bennett had gone to clean Blanche's cage, and while he was changing the water in her little cup and putting fresh newspapers on the floor, the bird was sitting on his shoulder. Blanche sometimes says words that you can really understand, like "Good-bye, pal" and "How ya doin'?" Dad seemed to get a kick out of Blanche, and he spent a long time taking videos of Blanche, Valerie, and Gretchen, who were busy sticking bread with raisins into their oven.

That night, though, I heard Dad say to Mom, "Two such beautiful women, isn't it a shame?" and then he said, "It's kind of sad, isn't it?"

Valerie and Gretchen's house is as nice as ours and they have a bigger deck in back. They're always doing things to their house and even said they were going to be putting in a swimming pool this summer. And they have a talking bird too. All the time we'd been over there, they were kidding around and laughing and seemed pretty happy to me. I was going to say something then, ask Dad why he said it was sad, but decided not to. I figured it was because they were gay and was glad Bennett wasn't around to hear him say it. Anyway, the telephone rang right then, and it was Kim again; she wanted me to come over and see a video of her playing a solo at her cousin's engagement party.

Mom handed me the telephone with a little smile and held up the little box of birthday candles she'd just found in a kitchen drawer. I wasn't sure she was smiling because Kim had called or she'd found the candles. Sometimes both of my parents are really hard to read.

19

The word got around school that my brother was building a gargantuan kite that was going to knock everyone's eyes out at graduation. Jeremy and Bennett had made a pact to keep its size, shape, and colors a deep secret. The particulars of the kite were like classified information I was just to keep buttoned up. Because the basement is where I have to do my saxophone practice, I was allowed to see it; there was no way they could keep me out. Bennett and Jeremy made me promise I wouldn't let anyone but Nolan get a look. And maybe Shearon, because he had a big wagon they'd need to get it to school.

I'd been watching it grow and now I admit I was pretty impressed. It was getting humongous, something you'd see at an airport, not in somebody's basement, a doghouse-size thing that took up half the space from the ping pong table to the ceiling, almost touching the track lights Dad had installed a couple of years ago. I said, "Wow! It's so big you could practically live in it!" which I could see pleased my brother, who said it would be even bigger when he got through with it, and made Jeremy give me a two-thumbs-up.

It was a Friday afternoon and Bennett and I were standing in the lobby of the school waiting for Mom. If it wasn't raining we would have been outside and nothing like what happened would have happened. Mom was taking Bennett to the mall to buy new shoes. She said she did not want to see his ratty old ones sticking out from under his cap and gown. I was getting new underwear and Mom was going to buy herself a dress "for the big occasion." She was a few minutes late and Jeremy and Nolan came running up when they saw us. Jeremy wanted Bennett to look around in the mall to see if he could find a strato-spool, cheap.

"What's that?" I asked.

"It's this wooden thing that holds the kite line," Jeremy explained, and just as he was describing it to me, Go-go and a few of his amigos appeared.

"Afraid to go out into the rain?" Go-go said to Bennett, in that razzing-spiky tone of voice, the minute he saw us. "'Fraid you're gonna get your *hair* messed up?"

I could feel myself getting into a hot lather. "We're getting a ride, going to the mall," I said, "if it's any of your biz." I wished I hadn't said it; why had I said it? It just popped out of my mouth.

"Gonna buy Bennett a new *dress*?" Go-go asked, and all the amigos just burst into leather-lunged laughs you could probably hear two floors away in the library.

Go-go had just opened his hall locker to put in some stuff and Jeremy took a step towards him to look inside. Maybe he was looking for stolen goods or maybe it was just curiosity, but it was a mistake. Next to Go-go Jeremy looked even shorter than he is. "Get off it, Go-go, leave my friend ALONE!" he piped up, surprising me and just about everybody.

Go-go's eyebrows moved up so far I thought they were

going to leave his head. "Your *friend*? I hear you and your *friend* are making a kite. *Sewing* a kite. Will the colors match your friend's *eyes*?" he snickered, and his groupies let out hoots and duck quacking sounds and eeeyooos and yeehaws. The amigos were circling us, reminding me of aliens surrounding a U. S. space ship. They looked as if they'd grown double size since lunch. I was backing away towards the door, saying, "C'mon, Bennett, c'mon guys, let's go!" but no one paid the slightest attention to me. Things were really heating up and I wished Mom would get here in a hurry.

Then Go-go said, "Maybe your friend is really your *girl*friend!" and Jeremy lost it. He lunged forward and grabbed everything he could get his hands on in Go-go's locker and started tossing the stuff—an old T-shirt, a baseball jacket, a couple of books, a sneaker, a bottle of water is what I saw as it sailed past me—and it went flying out all over the place, scattering on the hall floor in every direction.

The amigos—there were only three or four guys at this time, but it seemed all of a sudden like a hundred and fifty—started yelling, "Whooeee! Look at the dinky go! Go, go, go, itsy-bitsy, teensy-weensy Jeremidget!" mixed with whistles and a few dog barks.

"HEY!" Go-go yelled.

What came down next happened in such a hurry that I'm not sure whether it was Go-go or one of his amigo-buddies that started it. Jeremy got lifted into the air and held up there like a prize you'd win for knocking down bottles at a carnival, and then somebody said, "Let's see if Junior will fit in there," and the next thing that happened was that Jeremy was being swooped down from the air and pushed into Go-go's locker. His feet were kicking or trying to, his arms were being held down, his elbows pushed against his body and forced into this little space, stuffed like laundry into a place that was designed to hold no more than a couple of necessary school items of the type now littering the floor. Somebody's hand was on the side of Jeremy's head, his face was all blotched up in colors like a bruise that's fading, and his mouth was way open. Somehow, although we expected him to, he couldn't seem to get the yells and screams out.

All the noise was coming from the guys, although Bennett was yelling too, screaming, "Let him go! Let him GO!" at the top of his lungs. My brother started ripping off his jacket like he was going to really get into it—a definite first!

I guess it was no more than a minute that they held him in the locker, squeezed most of him in and were trying to close the door, and fiddling with the combination lock, intending, I guess, to keep him a crushed prisoner for I don't know how long, when the principal's secretary and Mr. Manheim came running, pulled him out, and broke things up.

Mr. Manheim looked highly steamed and kept asking Jeremy who'd started it, whose idea was it to scrunch Jeremy into Go-go's locker. The report would go to the principal, this was "serious," and there would be "major consequences," Mr. Manheim said. I wanted Jeremy to open his mouth and say the words, "Charles Mallis," which is Go-go's real name, but Jeremy said he wasn't sure who actually started the rumble. I knew he would have been only too happy to see Go-go expelled, if not put to death by lethal injection, but he didn't rat, although I think there are times it is absolutely necessary. I guessed it was because he was not so much a hero, but more because like me, and like Bennett, and like everyone else in school, he assumed there was no real winning when it came to the king of the school and his loyal band of buddies.

20

Since I got my new glove, my catching did not really get better, but whenever a ball landed in my mitt it felt solid and I felt solid too, and good about myself on second base or in the outfield. Somehow though, the Saturday after the locker incident, although I caught a few fly balls, ran some bases, and actually hit a triple, I wasn't really there. I kept thinking of Jeremy and what Go-go had done to him, and of course, Bennett was on my mind; in a way, my brother was the cause of the whole mess. After a while I started goofing up, swinging at balls I should have let go by and missing a really easy catch. I felt I was letting my team down.

About an hour into the game, I told the guys I had a sore shoulder and left the field to go home. It wasn't that much of a white lie because it was easier to say than trying to explain why I was really in no shape to catch, hit, or run. I got on my bike and pedaled home, thinking I'd just veg out for a change, play a few video games, and maybe just watch TV for the rest of the afternoon.

As I was about to glide down the driveway, an unfamiliar car pulled up in front of our house. About a second later, I reclassified it as a *familiar* car, very dark red, an SUV, with Illinois license plates. What was Jeremy's dad doing pulling up in front of our house? I stopped my bike to wave to him, and he waved back, but didn't stop to say anything, which was a new wrinkle; Mr. DeWitt is usually pretty jokey and friendly. I looked into the car windows, hoping he was dropping Nolan off, but no, he was alone, and he was heading for the front door. Before he even got to it, Dad opened it, and it was obvious he'd been expecting the visit. Nolan's Dad must have called while I was out at the ball field. Now they were shaking hands, and talking about the good weather and Mom's little row of tulips that were just starting to come out of the ground, and finally my father was showing Mr. DeWitt inside.

As soon as Dad saw me, he told me Valerie had called; she and Gretchen had work for me to do and I was to head over there as soon as I could. I guessed he wanted me out of the way, but knowing that gave me that much more incentive to hang around to hear whatever it was that had brought Nolan's father to our house.

I told Dad I'd just change my clothes, and headed upstairs to my usual listening spot, four steps from the top. Bennett was down in the basement working on his kite without Jeremy today, because as I suddenly remembered, all the DeWitt kids were going to the doctor for physical checkups or booster shots or something medical like that.

Dad invited Mr. DeWitt into the living room and offered him coffee. It's usually Mom who offers refreshment stuff, but she was working all weekend, and wouldn't get back till tomorrow night. Mr. DeWitt didn't want coffee, he politely told Dad.

There was some parent-to-parent type talk about the pictures of us that are all over the living room, and the painting of the flying birds over the fireplace, and then Nolan's dad got to the point. "Do you know what happened to Jeremy in school yesterday?" he asked. Dad, of course, was clueless.

"Some students tried to push Jeremy into a locker, and if it hadn't been for a teacher intervening, I honestly don't know how it would have ended."

I couldn't see Dad's face, but I knew exactly how it looked by the sound of his voice. His eyebrows must have really been up there. He hadn't been told, he said, he was surprised, actually *shocked*, that Bennett had never even mentioned it. They'd had breakfast and dinner together, and actually worked side by side sanding down some lawn furniture they were going to repaint, and Bennett hadn't said a *word*. Dad said he hoped that Bennett had had nothing to do with it, and there was sort of an exclamation point at the end of every one of his sentences.

Of course Bennett hadn't had anything to do with it, but now it turned out that's why Mr. DeWitt had come. He wanted to ask my brother why he thought those kids had turned on Jeremy. Was it because he was new, or because he was short, or was there some other reason he should know about?

"I can't get Jeremy to talk about it!" he said, sounding pretty stirred up. "He's up in his room, covered with Band-Aids and bruises, and he's not saying a word! His mother is really upset!"

Dad walked to the head of the basement stairs and yelled, "Bennett! Come up here for a minute, will you?"

And Bennett's voice came back, "In a minute, Dad! I'm just finishing something down here!"

Then Dad, louder, "*Now* Bennett! It's important!"

"I'm right in the middle of gluing!"

"Jeremy's father is here!" Dad bellowed then, and right away I heard my brother's feet come pounding up the stairs.

"Hi, Bennett," Mr. DeWitt said. "Working on your kite?" I had the feeling he'd been sitting with Dad in the living room, but now I could hear him get up; I could tell by the sound of the chair legs scraping along the floor. I moved down a step and peeked through the slats of the stair rail. Mr. DeWitt looked like he was expecting the national anthem to begin any minute, or something just as serious. His face looked sort of set, as if his right hand would zoom up and land over his heart. "How are you, Benny?"

Bennett was a little green around the gills—that's Mom's expression for anyone who looks clutched, sick, or wiped out. Also, nobody calls Bennett Benny; he hates that name. "I'm not a psychedelic drug," I heard him say the last time someone slipped up. It was a kid on the school bus, as I remember.

"I just came by to hear your version of the school fracas," Mr. DeWitt began, and it was said very low-key and friendly. I never heard the word 'fracas' before and wondered if it was some term they use a lot in Chicago.

"You never said a word about it!" Dad, on the other hand, sounded as if he had been kept out of the loop and was not only wired, but very, very hurt. My father likes to be in on everything, just like I do.

Bennett sort of shrugged, acting like it was no biggie. The truth is, he isn't much for bringing school tales home, the way I do. "Some of the guys thought they were being funny, that's all," he said, but he looked edgy, knowing very well he had just spoken one of the biggest understatements of all time.

"Why were they picking on my son, Bennett?" Mr. DeWitt persisted. "Why *Jeremy*?"

I moved down a few steps to get a better view. It went on like that, back and forth, with Bennett offering not the slightest scrap of real information, Mr. D. pacing around the living room, and Dad frowning at Bennett, at the floor, and just at the air in general. Bennett did say that Go-go was known around school for trouble and that he, Bennett, had been picked on plenty himself. Dad kept wanting to know why none of this had been reported to the "proper authorities" or discussed at home. There were a lot of moments of silence, and the upshot was that Mr. DeWitt said that he and Mrs. DeWitt would go to school first thing Monday morning "to get some nuts-and-bolts answers." He was not going to let it pass!

Before he left, he shook hands with Dad, told him that, thanks to Bennett, Jeremy had given up his stilts, called Bennett a fine young man, patted him on his shoulder. Then he said he hoped to straighten everything out before graduation and wished good luck with the "kite project." "It's all Jeremy talks about," he added.

It was about this time I was spotted by Dad, who reminded me to get over to Valerie and Gretchen's right this minute, and what did I think I was doing there on the stairs still in my messed-up clothes?

"And wash your face, for heaven's sakes!" he called

after me, as I ran upstairs. I figured he didn't want me to appear in the living room in front of a guest looking like I did, which is why I think I got away with not being grilled about my take on the locker incident. *Fracas.* I liked that word and let it hop around my head a few times as I went into the bathroom to wash up.

21

I worked the rest of the afternoon cleaning out Blanche's cage and hauling old books to the attic. Valerie and Gretchen were not only going to put in a swimming pool, but were also getting ready to paint their living room. Blanche had learned a couple of new phrases: "Lighten up, will you?" "It's party time!" and funniest of all, "Don't step in that!" which Gretchen said she had never heard before.

"Want a soda, Matthew?" Gretchen asked me about a few minutes later, and suddenly there was an echo. "Want a soda, want a soda?" Blanche squawked. Actually, she didn't even sound like a bird. She sounded like a loud, crabby person, like a voice in a cartoon show.

"I wouldn't mind one, thank you," I said to Valerie, with an eye on Blanche, expecting her to mimic, "I wouldn't mind one," but instead, she said, "I love you much-mucho, buddy!" and got us all laughing.

I think Blanche saved the day for me.

That afternoon in Valerie and Gretchen's attic I came across an old poster of Mickey Mantle, standing in the door of his restaurant. The poster had once belonged to Valerie's dad, she'd forgotten all about it, and said I was welcome to it. Mickey Mantle is my second-favorite hero after Sammy Sosa, so I was very interested in having it.

It looked a little frayed around the edges and a corner was torn off, but I figured I could take it home, tape the tears, and hang it on the door of our bedroom. Bennett had made a map of our state with a big X where our town is, but that had been up on the door for at least a year. I figured I could talk him into Mickey Mantle.

When I got home, though, he was in a mood. He was at the window of our room, probably waiting for the moon to pop out, although it was nowhere near dark. I showed him the poster and he shook his head. He said he didn't like it and didn't want to hang it *anywhere*. "I worked a week on that map," he said, when I suggested taking it down. "It stays where it is!"

"Come on, *Bennett*!" I begged and pleaded. I know I was overreacting, but all the way home, I'd kept picturing Mickey Mantle on the door. He'd be the first thing I'd see when I woke up in the morning, instead of Bennett's boring map.

"No!" he repeated.

I suggested he move some of Frankie's pictures then, and we could paste the poster on the wall over the bureau. I thought he was going to take a swipe at me then, even for suggesting it. "Have you *lost* it, Matthew?" he yelled.

"Lighten up!" I said, sounding like Blanche.

That night we went to bed without saying another word to each other, and I knew it was more than the poster getting to him. It was Jeremy's dad. He figured there'd be trouble ahead, and so did I.

All day Monday in school, I imagined that any minute, *bad news* would happen. Although I knew Mr. and Mrs.

DeWitt had come to school to talk to the principal, I didn't know what the results would be. I sensed what Mr. Gold says dogs feel before an earthquake: an electric sizzle in the air. I didn't see Go-go at lunch, but a few of the amigos were huddled together at one end of the cafeteria, never a good sign.

Amigo is a Spanish word for friend, but these guys were not Spanish and as far as being friends—to each other or even to Go-go—I wouldn't bet on that either. Actually, one or two were from a country where people speak Spanish or maybe Portuguese, but the rest of the guys were American troublemakers with an attitude and fat shoulders. If I had to use one word to describe them, I'd say "scuzzy," but one word is not enough. Another word I'd use would be "NG," which is what Bennett calls them—but not when they're around to hear him.

They were in a bunch and without Go-go, which was suspicious right there. I thought maybe he'd cut school or was being grilled by the principal. Maybe, if we were lucky, he'd come down with some creeping crud that would sideline him for the rest of the year!

Wishful thinking. The good news was that he was in trouble. The bad news came the next morning, on the school bus.

22

Bennett had worked so late putting finishing touches on his kite the night before that I had a hard time getting him up. By the time he and I ran out of the house to catch the bus, we could see it already rounding the corner to leave our street. Luckily, the bus driver saw us through his rearview and stopped long enough for us to run like crazy and get aboard. Ordinarily, this would not have made the news, except that as soon as we got on, I saw something that spooked me: two of the amigos were sitting one behind the other in aisle seats. *What were these two guys doing here today?*

I knew they lived somewhere in our neighborhood, but unless there was snow a foot deep or hailstones the size of golf balls coming out of the sky, they were on their bikes or scooters every school day. Needless to say, they didn't have the sort of baggage Bennett and I seem to have to carry back and forth day in, day out. In fact, Bennett's backpack was so full he was carrying a notebook stuffed with papers in his hands and I had my usual gear plus my saxophone.

Right away, I saw trouble. "Hi, Bennett," one of the boys said, in a voice that went too high and too loud, like a lady opera singer's. Bennett, of course, kept moving, and I was right behind him. For some reason, maybe because the weather report was rain, the bus was as crowded as it gets on rainy days. All the seats in the front looked taken.

"Hi, Bennett!" Now both of the guys sang, loud and louder. Bennett was sort of jammed in the aisle and I couldn't see his face, but could see the back of his neck over his shirt collar, and it was getting pink.

"Cut it out," I said to the amigos, trying to sound fierce, but they ignored me.

"Hey, Auntie Bennett," they were calling now. "What you got in your backpack, a pair of high heels and your lipstick?"

There were laughs left and right and now it was my own face I felt burning up. "CUT THAT OUT!" I yelled, louder this time. It's as if I hadn't said a word; they kept right on, chanting, "Auntie Benn-ett, Auntie Benn-ett!"

Some other kids joined in and then, although I knew it wasn't everybody, it sounded as if every kid on the bus was yelling "Benn-ett! Benn-ett!"

All this time the bus hadn't moved; the bus driver was waiting for everyone to sit down. "Find a seat in the rear," he yelled. "I'm not moving until everyone's got a seat!"

Bennett and I kept trying to move back and I realized we'd have to squeeze in next to someone, but no one moved to make room.

Then one of the amigos yelled, "Hey, Bennett, you fruitcake! Your sweetheart got Go-go in trouble. Are you and him getting *married*?" and I realized this was why they were on the bus today. To get even. "You two are just a pair of lovebirds," the other amigo chimed in, and a whole bunch of kids yelled, "Ooooh, Bennett! Ooooh, sweetie pie!" My brother spun around and I got really scared; the look on his face was murder. If his hands weren't full of stuff I'm pretty sure he would have thrown a punch.

The bus driver was looking in his rearview mirror and yelling at everybody to be quiet and get a seat. "What's going on back there?" he kept saying.

Now, amigo number one cried, "Hey, isn't someone going to get up and give the lady a seat?" and he got up himself, pretending to make room. That's when all hell broke loose: as he lifted himself up, he gave my brother a shove, Bennett slipped and fell, and the notebook he was holding spun out of his hands.

Papers went in every direction. Bennett's reports, notes, assignments, drawings, whatever, went first into the air and then to the floor of the bus, and everybody started yelling, stamping feet, laughing and whistling, like this was the best show they'd ever seen. My brother was scrambling to pick himself and his paper trail off the floor and I was trying to help him, when the bus driver left his seat and came marching down the aisle. He was wearing a big leather jacket with studs, the kind you'd see on a member of a motorcycle gang, and he looked like he meant business. Everyone quieted down.

He saw Bennett down on his hands and knees. "Who pushed you?" he asked. I don't know how he knew Bennett hadn't just tripped or something, but he *knew*. Bennett didn't answer. "Who knocked you down?" the bus driver persisted. He was looking left and right, but the amigos had shut up and now managed to look as innocent as the most well-behaved members of a new kindergarten class. Looking at them, I felt as if a bubble was growing inside me. I wanted my brother to tell the bus driver who'd done this, right now. I wanted the driver to report the amigos to the principal, to their parents, to the superintendent of schools or the police if possible, but Bennett, still on hands and knees, kept picking up his stuff off the bus floor and not saying a word.

"C'mon, who did this to you?" the bus driver asked one more time, and inside me, I felt like the bubble was pushing against my vital organs, shutting off my air supply.

Bennett, say something!

"You're not gonna tell me?" the driver said and I could see by the way his mouth was stretched to show all his top teeth that he was plenty annoyed. "I'm listening, kid. *Who?*"

Just like Jeremy, I guess Bennett decided not to rat.

That's when the bubble went *pop* and I made one of the biggest mistakes of my life.

"*He* did," I said, pointing to the amigo who had shoved my brother and knocked him down, "*that's* the guy."

I could hear sort of a general hum all around me after I said it. It sounded like a big *oh-oh* that nobody was actually saying, but was hanging in the air like a rustle in the trees in a jungle. *Oh-oh*, *oh-oh*, *oh-oh*.

Call me a snitch, a squealer or a tattletale; call me a rat fink, or whatever you like. If they hadn't made fun of Bennett, hadn't called him names and made him seem like a freak of nature, I probably would have kept my mouth closed, but I just couldn't. Could *not*! I was in danger of suffocating!

He did, *he did*, *he did*. I'd only said it once but it was like an echo in my head.

The bus driver didn't hesitate. He pointed at the amigo and in a Frankenstein voice, said, "Okay, you. Get off the bus." There was such a sudden hush now you would have thought a curtain had gone up, which in a way, it had.

"I said, get off the bus. Now!" the bus driver said again, and for a minute, I felt as good as I've ever felt in my life. The amigo, with his face looking as if someone had flattened it with a mallet, pulled his backpack on, grumbled a bad word, heaved himself out of his seat and with a killer look at me, made his way down the aisle, and headed out the door of the bus.

23

Three hours later, I was sitting at lunch with Nolan, hardly able to take a bite out of my chicken sandwich, when another one of Go-go's pals came over to our table. This was one of the guys who'd stood by cheering while his buddies tried to stuff Jeremy into the locker. I stopped breathing, knowing whatever was coming, was coming this minute. I saw Nolan drop his slice of pizza just as the amigo's hand came down on my shoulder. I felt his fingers squeezing, and it was like the top of my body was caught in the grip of a flying reptile. Any minute the large and small bones in my shoulder would be crushed into bits. In his other prehistoric hand, he had a big plastic bottle of orange soda he was taking gulpy sips out of.

"Hey, little weasel," he said, and of course, he was talking to me. "I hear you got Ethan thrown off the bus this morning."

I didn't know the bus guy's name was Ethan, which seems too good a name for anyone like that kid. I had a friend in camp named Ethan, a really good guy and until this minute, liked the name pretty much.

"So, Ethan was late for school and got detention. What do you say to that, weasel?"

I didn't have anything to say to that or to anything else this pinhead bully was going to want to discuss. I began to get up out of my chair, but his hand on my shoulder kept me pinned to my seat.

"And your buddy's parents caused Go-go to get suspended for a week, along with Spitz, Rod, Muzz, and Bryson."

"Right," Nolan spoke up, surprising me. "That's what you all get for trying to stuff my brother into a locker." He was actually pointing a finger at the amigo, which I consider a heroic act of bravery. "He wasn't even *bothering* you."

"I wasn't even talking to you, friend of weasel," the amigo said, pointing the bottle of soda at Nolan. He took his hand off my shoulder and moved it to the back of my chair. He began rocking the chair back and forth, back and forth.

"Cut that out!" I said, and no surprise, he ignored me, tipping me so far back my feet were off the floor and I was staring up at the lights on the ceiling. If he let go my head would smash to the floor and I'd be a goner.

"Did you hear him?" Nolan piped up. "*Cut it out!*"

"What did you say?" The amigo stopped rocking my chair and pushed me back into upright position. I was saved while he focused on Nolan.

Nolan had picked up his slice and was about to bite into it. "We're having our lunch, if you don't mind," he said. "Get lost," he added.

The amigo's eyes bulged. "You need to be taught a lesson, friend of weasel," he said, and he swooped his orange soda bottle into the air over Nolan's head like he was the Statue of Liberty. With his other hand, he tipped back *his* chair, and now Nolan was almost horizontal, his feet in the air and kicking.

With Nolan a prisoner in midair, the amigo tipped the orange soda bottle and let it pour in a big orange stream right on his face. The soda splattered over Nolan's hair, his shirt and the front of his pants. He was soaked orange practically head to foot.

"HEY!" he screamed, and the amigo rocked him back and forth a couple of times before setting the chair back on its four legs. He was letting out laughs that came out like a sound track for a slash-and-burn movie. Jumping up, Nolan let out a few bad words and looked like he intended to pick up his chair and throw it at the amigo, but the amigo laughed, said, "Don't forget to recycle," dropped the empty bottle on Nolan's head, turned, and walked away. Two teachers who were standing in the doorway of the cafeteria glanced our way, but by the time they got a real look at Nolan, the amigo had disappeared, and Nolan was wiping his face, hair, and the front of his shirt with a napkin. They must have thought he'd spilled the soda on himself.

That night, *Mrs.* DeWitt called. Mom turned quiet, listening to Nolan's mother. My ears went up. I heard her saying, "I never heard a word about it," and then she looked my way. I knew the questions would start flying in my direction as soon as she got off the phone.

Sure enough: "Orange soda?" she asked. "Who would dare do such a thing?"

I ducked and hedged. I didn't want to get into the bus

story. I didn't want to talk about my brother. I was worried through and through as it was that they'd find out about him.

"There are some real jerks in school," I told Mom. "They cause trouble all the time." I was telling the truth, one hundred percent. Okay, maybe only ninety-five percent. Mom is very smart and I don't think she was really buying it. She was looking at me with very suspicious eyes.

"Is there any reason they'd be picking on Nolan and Jeremy?" she asked me. What could I say to that? I shrugged, and then relaxed, because she got busy looking for a soup ladle or something and said maybe it was just junior high school spring fever. She hoped the teachers were "supervising adequately" and that this was the last such incident. And, considering what was going on in some American schools, maybe orange soda was not that serious a crime.

In fact, at dinner, when she and Dad talked about it, he said he thought Mrs. DeWitt might be overreacting. "Boys will be boys," he added. He guessed the DeWitt boys were newcomers being "tested." I noticed Bennett was being very quiet, unusually interested in his salad, to which he was giving his complete and wholehearted attention.

I tried to get his eye, to send the message that he could count on me to be a clam, but he was going at his tomatoes and lettuce like he'd never tasted such a delicacy before. He never once looked up.

When Dad reminded me to go downstairs and practice, that graduation was only two weeks away, for once I was happy to leave the table. It might have been the stress, because I really blew into the saxophone with my heart and soul that night. I gave it my all, and when I finished and went upstairs, it was almost like I got my reward: the poster of Mickey Mantle was hanging on the inside of the door to our room. Bennett had fixed the little rips and tears with tape and it looked almost new.

"I changed my mind," he explained, while I stood there for about five minutes admiring it.

"It looks cool," I told him. He'd rolled up his map of the state and stuck it under the bed.

"I guess it's not that bad," he said, and then added that seeing as I was finished blowing my notes, he guessed he'd go down to the garage and do a last minute check on the kite. It had outgrown the basement and been moved there along with the ping pong table.

"We're going to do a test run Friday night if there's enough wind."

"At *night*?"

"I *was* trying to keep it a surprise."

"Can I come?"

"I guess so," Bennett said, with a shrug. "Now Jeremy wants to bring his whole family and I promised Shearon *he* could come."

I would honestly say that when Bennett even said the word 'kite' something happened to him. His eyes got a Christmas-morning look and his voice got more weighty and potent, as if the kite were already high in the sky and people were up and cheering. He was jumpy too, the way people are when their favorite player is at bat with bases loaded. It was as if Bennett turned into a bigger-than-life blowup just at the thought of what was about to happen. He admitted he dreamed about the kite just about every night. "Just don't go blabbing it to the immediate world, okay?" he said, forgetting most everyone had already gotten wind of it.

It's not the Olympics, I thought, but I said, "I won't," and thanked him again for hanging the poster, telling him our room now looked downright *excellent.*

24

As soon as I walked through the door at home the next afternoon, Mom got me helping to clean up the downstairs bathroom. This was kite preview night and she does a general swab-down and fresh towels whenever company is on its way, even if it's only the DeWitts. Although all three of the triplets had colds or were coming down with them, they said they wouldn't miss the kickoff. Their parents wouldn't miss it either, so of course they were on the guest list too.

Bennett had also invited Shearon. Shearon has this big wagon thing with rubber wheels he calls a dolly. It would transport the kite to the park, which was one reason Bennett asked him to come. Of course, Bennett and Jeremy could have just as easily carried it, so I think the main idea was that Bennett hoped he and Shearon were still friends. I was sure he wanted to keep that buddy thing going.

I was putting out the new dinosaur soap when I heard Dad come in. He was early, said he'd had a hard day, his shoulder was killing him, but he was definitely up for the launch. On the way home, though, he'd heard the weather report, a possibility of thunderstorms.

Bennett was on his way to the garage to cover the kite with a sheet so there'd be a big, dramatic ta-da when he whipped it off, so I knew he'd heard Dad. I also guessed this was one of the two days of the whole year the weather just had to be right, so I said, "The TV report is wrong half the time," and my brother picked up on that immediately and said, "Yeah, the forecast is never right." I really hoped tonight wouldn't be totally ruined for him.

As it turned out, the weatherman was wrong, but what Bennett saw when he jumped up to look out the window five or six times during dinner, was not lightning and thunder, not rain, but fog. There was this mist so thick you would have thought we were all at sea, and the worst part of the weather was that there was no wind. Dad said the air looked like you could practically walk on it, but it was still early and the sky might yet clear up.

Shearon arrived first, rolling this dolly thing down the driveway, saying there was no wind but the fog wasn't all that bad, but the DeWitts came a few minutes later, with a different story. They'd nearly hit a parked car when they turned the corner of their street, but hoped the mist would lift soon. In the meantime, they'd brought ice cream in all kinds of flavors like white chocolate mousse, blueberry swirl, and chocolate-pecan, to help celebrate. Mrs. DeWitt helped Mom stuff it all into the freezer. Nobody said anything about the locker incident or orange soda, so I began to relax, thinking everything was going to be cool.

Bennett was practically *glowing.*

Before ice cream, though, Jeremy said we ought to have the unveiling. "Unveiling," I guessed, was another word imported from Chicago, but it meant everybody would now get to see Bennett take the sheet off the kite. Even though I'd seen it in the basement a million times, beginning from its being just a couple of strips of colored nylon stuff and a bunch of sticks, I hadn't seen it one hundred percent assembled, so it was still a mind-blowing moment.

Bennett and Jeremy led the way.

My brother was talking a mile a minute, about how he was sure it was going to go higher than the water tower at the other end of town, and how he thought it would definitely make the newspaper, maybe even page one. "Maybe TV too!" He didn't know of anyone in the whole state who'd ever built a kite this big, and for sure, nobody had ever thought of flying one on graduation day. Everyone would take pictures of it, it would go in next year's yearbook, it would make history! *The rainbow kite would never be forgotten!* I hadn't seen him this charged as long as I could remember. The night I heard him crying seemed like ancient history. It wasn't that my brother was bragging, but I could feel he was what Mom once called walking tall, and that, for Bennett, was a new and really unusual thing.

Jeremy too, if you could say walking tall. He'd grown a little bit—at least, he insisted he had—but he was still no taller than me. Now, though, he was puffed up and telling everybody who would listen that the kite had been his idea in the first place and if it hadn't been for him, this could never have happened, and so on. Mr. DeWitt put a hand on Jeremy's shoulder and said he deserved credit, yes, and it was a creation that was definitely one hundred percent fifty-fifty! I got a look at Jeremy's face when his dad said that and he looked pretty happy. At the time, I thought Mr. DeWitt was really a very cool dad.

We had to go single file to the basement because the steps are narrow, and we were like a little army clattering down the stairs. Then, through the basement and into the garage, where Dad switched on the overhead lights, which turned the place bright as daylight. Bennett and Jeremy had moved the kite from the basement to put it all together and now it was obvious why; the thing under the sheet was about as wide as a car and almost as tall as Jeremy, and could never have gotten outside through the basement door. We sort of stood in a circle around the table, staring at the sheet, all talking and kidding around at once, when Mom suddenly said, "Sshh. Just a minute everybody—did you hear something?"

We shushed for a second, but then one of Nolan's triplet brothers, Adam, sneezed like three times in a row. When his mother handed him a tissue, he blew his nose, and when he stopped sneezing and blowing, he coughed a couple of times. After he finally quieted down, we listened for a minute, but all we heard was the sound of the TV somebody had left on upstairs.

Now finally, Bennett said, "Is everyone ready?" and it was what you call a Moment in Time. We all stepped back like we were ready for someone to fire off a rocket, then he and Jeremy counted back from ten. "—three, two, one—SLIDE OFF!" Jeremy said, and he and Bennett carefully tugged the sheet off the kite. There it was and I'll say this: it really knocked us out.

Not only was it huge and looked like something that had come out of a next-century high-tech factory instead of our basement, but the colors, well, they were zinging, flashy, they were *hot.* Roy B. Giv, I remembered, and the strips were sewed together straight as rulers—well, almost—and to this day, I don't know how my brother and Jeremy managed to pull the whole thing off. Whenever people say "work of art," my brother's kite is what I think of. Anyhow, it was a showstopper.

Dad said he couldn't believe his eyes. This kite belonged in a museum, not a garage. He was smiling big smiles, and I guessed he figured Bennett's problems were over. Maybe he figured his talks finally hit the mark. Mr. DeWitt said he was at a loss for words but then found some, like "great job," "incredible," "You'll wow 'em" and so on, and Nolan asked if he could touch it. I was afraid if any of the triplets got too close they'd sneeze all over it, but they kept a respectful distance. Mrs. DeWitt said she'd never expected anything like this, and wished she'd brought her camera. Shearon said, "It's an ineffable accomplishment!" and I figured "ineffable" was an eighth-grade vocabulary word. His rooter whistle summed the whole thing up.

Dad said he was lucky to have a camcorder to videotape graduation and long after the kite was gone, it would be immortalized on tape. That little speech got Mr. DeWitt to say, "Hear ye, hear ye!" and Mom to put an arm around Bennett's shoulder. Bennett looked as if he himself was ready to lift off the ground and fly.

Then Mom, all smiles, suggested we go upstairs, have some ice cream. "By the time we're through, maybe the fog will have lifted." She was all upbeat, looking so pleased and proud she was practically bouncing. I think she thought Bennett's kite would lead to his making a zillion friends, getting umpteen scholarships, maybe becoming some kind of five-star engineer. Just a guess, but I know Mom.

We followed her upstairs, and while she was rummaging through drawers, searching for the ice cream scoop, we heard a noise outside, as if something had been smacked up against the front door. It was the sound the newspaper makes when the paperboy manages to make a direct hit, but this whap was louder and more ear-popping.

"Wait—didn't you hear that?" Mom asked, and this time, we'd all heard it. We got very still, waiting.

I'd been holding a spoon in my hand and now put it down as if it had slipped, although it hadn't; it's as if someone had yelled "Mayday!" or maybe it was the look on Bennett's face, or just a feeling I had. I think I'd been waiting for something really awful, something worse than orange soda to happen since I'd ratted on the amigo on the school bus. I froze.

And although the fog had lifted and the sky was clear, and later Bennett said he'd never seen the moon so "militantly bright," I never did taste the white chocolate mousse ice cream. It was that thump, that loud thwack that turned everything upside down that night, changed everything from great to horrific in about as long as it took for Dad to say, "I'll take a look outside," and Mr. DeWitt to say, "I'll go with you."

25

We all followed, of course. That is, we stood in the doorway while Dad switched on the light over the front door and he and Mr. DeWitt looked at what somebody had left on the doorstep. "Left on the doorstep" is what we thought at first, but later, we realized it had been *thrown* at the house, had bounced off the door and landed on the doormat. That's what made the smack-thump sound we heard, and whatever it was looked like it was wrapped in a few of those white plastic bags Mom carries groceries home in.

First Dad and Mr. DeWitt looked up and down the street to see if whoever had thrown the thing was still around, but by this time it was pretty dark and the street looked pretty quiet and empty. Dad picked up the sack and Mom stopped him from bringing it inside. I could see she was very nervous, but not nearly as clutched as I was. Let me put it this way: I was terrified. This had to do with the school bus, for sure. "Don't open it!" I said to Dad and when it came out like sort of a warning bark, Dad and Mr. DeWitt's head swiveled in my direction. They looked at me as if I had gone suddenly loco.

"Why not?" Dad said.

I stared at the sack, which anyone would say looked like an innocent little bag containing a shoe or a couple of potatoes. To me it looked like dynamite. I didn't answer.

"Why *not*, Matthew?" Dad asked again. He had the sack in his hand and was sort of holding it out, away from his body. Mr. DeWitt had taken a step away from Dad, I noticed. They were both looking at me like I knew something. Of course, I did. Whatever was in that sack had to do with Bennett and had to be *not* good.

All this time, Mom and Mrs. DeWitt had been in the doorway, bunched together, and the kids behind and in front of them, pushing to see what was going on. Now, all of a sudden, everyone was outside, sort of in a circle around Dad, who had his fingers around the top of the sack.

"We have to see what someone left us," he said. My father is very brave, nothing like me.

"But what if it *explodes*?" I said. I saw DANGER written all over this situation. I wished we were all inside peacefully eating ice cream, wished it were yesterday or last Saturday at the ball field. I'd made an amazing catch with my new glove, then ran a triple that day. That seemed very long and far away.

Mom looked scared to bits. I guess I take after *her*. "Maybe Matthew is right—" she was saying to Dad.

"Well, what am I going to do, just throw it away?"

"Call the police," Mom said. "I'll go call 911."

"Lydia! Call the police because someone left a little sack on our doorstep?" It sounded sensible to me, but he made it sound like a totally ridiculous thing to do.

All this time, Bennett and Jeremy were standing by, a pair of silent statues. I had no idea what they were thinking, but I figured my brother's wheels must really be turning. The thing with Bennett is it's hard to know what's going on in his head. I did notice he stepped back when Dad started to unwrap the thing, but of course, we all did. There was a sack within a sack within a sack, but finally, Dad turned the thing upside down, and what fell out was a huge, furry black rat, dead, with one eye closed and one half-open. You could see its pointed teeth even in the dark light, and its paws. It was sort of curled up, almost like it was sleeping. It had a tail that looked like black leather, and it had been half cut off.

Mom screamed. Everybody else cried out; I saw Bennett's hands fly up to his mouth. Mr. DeWitt put his arm around Mrs. DeWitt, and I started feeling barfy, but the person who really freaked was Nolan. "NO! NO!" he kept yelling. "A rat! They killed an innocent rat!" Nolan loves animals, especially rats, and I know what he was thinking. And he was shaking, head to foot. His mom got all that right away.

"It's not Felix, darling," she said, and went over to put an arm around him, but he was looking bad. Nolan looked as if he was running a fever, which in fact he was.

"It could have been! If they got hold of Felix—*it could have been him!*" Nolan went completely out of control, shaking top to bottom.

"I think it's time to call the police," Mom said. "We have a good reason, now, don't we?"

About a second later, we got a better reason.

"LOOK!" Shearon saw it first. I suppose we'd missed it because of the rat. Now we stood together in the driveway, all of us, staring at the garage door—and the basketball hoop over it.

They'd hung a ladies' brassiere from the hoop.

And they'd spray painted the word FAGGOT in black letters across the door of the garage that Bennett had painted white just a couple of months ago. Each letter was almost as big as I am. I think if you stood a mile away and there was poor visibility, you still couldn't miss it.

26

FAGGOT

I kept looking at the big letters on the garage door to convince myself this was actually happening. I wasn't going to wake up in my bed any time soon and find I'd had a terrible dream. The fog had lifted and I felt a breeze, a few drops of rain, and it was all real, one hundred percent.

There was a general hyper-commotion with everybody shell-shocked, including me. Mom was holding on to Dad, Dad was trying to calm her down, Mrs. DeWitt said she thought Nolan was feeling sick and Jeremy seemed so upset they thought they'd better leave. She whispered something to Mr. DeWitt and then he said they wouldn't wait around for the police unless Dad felt we needed them to stay. Adam was sneezing and coughing and in-between asking, "What's 'faggot' mean?" I couldn't believe he'd never heard that word in Chicago; it seemed I'd known all my life what it meant, and seeing it in spray paint written all over our garage was making me even sicker than before.

I looked for Bennett, but he'd suddenly disappeared. I guessed he'd run up to our room. I wanted to run up there too, but at the moment, Dad had his hand on top of my arm and was holding on. If he needed someone to lean on, for sure I was the wrong person. I was really shivering now and this time it wasn't even cold outside.

"This is about Bennett," he said. I wasn't sure if he was asking me or telling me, so I didn't say anything. "Bennett," Dad repeated. "Oh, Bennett!" and he closed his eyes, squeezed them shut as if he never intended to use them again, and he turned his back to the garage door. The look on his face scared the life out of me.

The DeWitts piled into their car, sort of quietly, except for one of the triplets, I'm not sure which one, who was coughing up a storm. Before she climbed into the seat next to Mr. DeWitt, Mrs. DeWitt went over to Mom and put both arms around her, and said something I couldn't hear. Almost as soon as Mrs. DeWitt climbed into the car, it pulled away from the curb, and the last thing I saw was Nolan, who had opened the window on his side to tell me he'd see me in school Monday. He yelled something else at me, and I think it was about the police. Maybe it was "The police will throw them in jail!" but I couldn't be sure.

Shearon said he thought he'd better go too, but would leave his dolly for as long as Bennett needed it.

Then Mom, Dad, and I went inside. I expected Dad to slap walls, to lose it, maybe even to yell about "thugs," "delinquents," and what god-awful things were going on in the world today, but none of that happened. Instead, Dad sank into his usual chair in the living room, leaned forward and then back and then forward again, sort of rocking back and forth. Then he put his head in his hands, covering his face, while Mom went to find the telephone. She'd misplaced it.

Maybe the little delay gave Dad enough time to think, because when she said, "Oh, here it is!" and pulled the phone out from under the newspapers on the table in the hall, Dad said, "Lyd, wait a minute. Let's just talk about this first."

His voice sounded deep, like it was coming from a cave.

Mom had the telephone in her hand and a what-do-you-mean look on her face.

"Let's talk to Bennett first," Dad said. He got up from his chair the way Grandpa sometimes does, as if there are rocks in his pockets weighing him down. Dad used both hands to lift himself out of the chair and made his way to the stairs. He called Bennett's name loud and louder, and when there was no answer, turned to me. "Go upstairs and tell your brother we want to speak to him," he said.

My brother was lying facedown on his bed, the Nirvana tape blaring. "Dad wants to talk to you," I told him, and for a minute he didn't move. "Bennett!" I said. "Did you hear me?"

My brother turned over and looked at me but his eyes looked bottled up, like he didn't see me at all. He had those red rings around them and a big gouged wrinkle where his pillow had scrunched up his cheek. He didn't say a word, just got up, ran into the bathroom, leaned over the toilet, and threw up.

27

Now the telephone was ringing. One ring, two, three; it was obvious no one at our house was in the mood to pick it up. From the top of the stairs, I could hear Mom's voice on the machine: "Please leave your name and number and we'll get back to you . . ." and a click. The caller had hung up. I'd turned off Nirvana; no reason to get Dad even more upset; my parents are not Nirvana fans. Bennett was still in the bathroom, now the door was closed and water was running. I guessed he'd gone into the shower.

"Matthew? Bennett?" Dad's voice was now at loudest pitch.

I stood at the top of the stairs and yelled down that Bennett was taking a shower.

Which brought Dad running up the stairs, Mom following. "Now? He's taking a shower NOW?" Dad knocked on the bathroom door. He used the knuckles of his right hand and then, as if they weren't working right, his left hand. Mom stood a few feet away, leaning against the door to Dad's office, her hands clasped in front of her like she was ready for a prayer service. Her eyes were definitely wet, but not exactly crying. Sort of on the verge. The phone was ringing again.

It seemed years went by before Bennett opened the door and stepped out of the bathroom. He had a towel wrapped around his waist and another one wrapped like a turban around his head.

Weird as it may sound, the sight of Bennett seemed to send Dad some odd bolt from the blue. He came out with the strangest, the most unexpected thing. The first words that popped out of his mouth were, "Get that towel off your head! For God's sake, what are you doing with a towel wrapped around your head, like a, like a—" and then he stopped cold, like someone had pushed a mute button on the world's remote control.

Bennett stammered, "My hair is wet," as if he had to come up with an excuse for twisting a towel around his head, like it was breaking some law. Right away I guessed Dad thought it made Bennett look like a girl and Bennett knew it, although *I* thought he looked like a genie in a cartoon show about the Arabian nights. A little dorky, maybe, but not swishy in the least.

Now Mom looked even more upset. "What is your *problem*?" she asked Dad, and then held both her hands up to the ceiling, saying, "That's not what's important here, is it? IS IT? We have to call the police!"

Dad did not look at Mom. "Do you have any idea who wrote 'faggot' on the garage door?" he asked Bennett and of course, Bennett had a very, very good idea, but he'd leaned over and was busy unwrapping his head. He didn't answer.

"Did you hear what I *asked* you?" Dad said while Bennett was rubbing the towel all over his hair and still not answering. Dad was simmering. Any minute, he'd hit a wall. Sure enough, he raised his hand and slapped the one nearest the bathroom door. *Whack.* Bennett jumped.

I think I did too. The towel my brother had wrapped his head in dropped to a heap on the floor. A blue towel corpse is the creepy thing that came flying into my head; it looked so *dead*, as if someone had killed it.

Dad kicked it out of the way and followed Bennett into our room. He lowered his voice, "And why? Why, Bennett? Can you please, please tell me *why*?"

He was acting as if it was Bennett's fault.

My brother sat on his bed, staring at the floor. The silence went on and on. Mom stood in the doorway, biting her lip, and I think I was up against the closet door, wishing I was anywhere else but here. On the other hand, no matter how hideous, I didn't want to miss what was coming next.

"Tell me *who*. Tell me *why*," Dad kept saying.

"Give him a minute," Mom said. "Can't you see how upset he is?"

Dad stood silent. We all did. If an ant had crawled across the lawn I think we would have heard it. It felt as if even the world had stopped whirling around the sun.

Dad's face and voice changed. Slapping the wall always does that, cools him off. "I'm not mad at you," he now said to my brother. It was a new, soft-pedal approach and I guess he meant it when he said it. "But you must know who would do this to you. Don't you, son?"

Bennett looked up from the floor.

"Why you, Bennett?" Dad persisted.

I was the scared one now. The best thing about my brother is that he doesn't like to lie, but it's the worst thing about him too. I pictured the word FAGGOT on the garage door again. How I felt this minute was, they could have spray painted DOOM right underneath it, if he went ahead and told the truth. And it looked as if Bennett was actually about to come clean.

Sure enough. "I'm gay," he said, just like that. It came out really quiet. Like a whisper at a funeral. "I'm queer, Dad."

Amazing. The words didn't choke him. There were no aftershocks; not even the lightning and thunder the weatherman had predicted. My brother didn't collapse or scream, or throw himself down to the floor. The moon didn't send any special beams or praise through the window. All that happened was that one single tear dripped out of Mom's eye; I caught it before she wiped it away.

And then, Dad surprised me again. Floored me, is more like it. He let out this turned-up pretend laugh. "That's ridiculous, Bennett. You may think you are, but you're not. NO! You're just a boy. Still a kid. You're no queer! You just have to stop acting like one. Don't give people that *impression*. We'll get you to see someone. Someone to help you work through it. You'll be fine, you'll see."

Then Dad sat next to Bennett and put his arm around his naked shoulders. "In fact, I don't really see any reason to call the police about this, I really don't."

Mom broke in. She'd found a tissue and was squeezing it against one eye. "What are you *saying*? A dead rat, a hate message and you're going to let whoever did this *get away with it*?"

"Why advertise it, Lydia? It'll be all over the newspapers, everyone in town will know, and then, just think, THINK, Bennett, what it will mean for you in school? And maybe in *life*! Don't you agree, Lydia? Why draw attention to it? Don't you see what I'm saying?"

28

There were more words between my parents, turned-up and hot, but my mother lost the fight. No one called the police. Instead, Mom went downstairs to make herself a "killer cup of tea" and a few minutes later, we heard Dad leave the house. I looked out the window in time to see him in his car, backing out of the driveway.

"Where do you suppose he's going?" I asked my brother. My heart was beating so loud I thought he could hear it. It was pretty late by this time, and the rain was really coming down.

But Bennett was not in a talking mood. He'd gotten in his pajamas and said he was going into Dad's office to do some homework on the computer. He left me alone in our room to worry my head off. I won't go into all the terrible ideas that were surging through my brain cells. Of course I wished Dad was right: he'd find a good shrink for Bennett and he'd be cured of being gay. He'd make new friends in high school, Go-go and his buddies would lay off all of us, and everything would be great at home, the way it was before. Down deep though, I thought, *no way.*

A while later, Mom came back upstairs, and I heard her asking Bennett if he wanted to come down to the kitchen for some of the ice cream that was still "ready and waiting" in the freezer. He didn't. Then she came to the door of my room. She was holding a mug of tea and asking me if I wanted to try some more of the white chocolate mousse or blueberry flavors the DeWitts had brought. For once in my life, I didn't want ice cream.

"Where did Dad go?" I asked her, but she shrugged. Dad *always* told Mom where he was going, even if it was to the garage to get gas. Could Dad possibly have gone for good? Now Mom could see my face, and took a guess at what was happening in my head, because she quickly said, "He hasn't gone very far, Matthew. I think he just had to cool off. He said he'd be back in a half hour."

Then she sat in my desk chair, looked into her tea, and said that even though she and Dad disagreed about certain issues, the thing they were both dedicated to completely and absolutely was the welfare of their two boys. "Your father loves you both dearly," she said, looking up at me, and she wanted to know if I was aware of that. I told her I was. "I want Bennett not to be angry at his father," she said then, but what could I say to that? I asked her if she thought a shrink would fix the problem and make Bennett all right. "Bennett IS all right," Mom said, and gave me a smile that reminded me of the way she looks in a photograph she had taken next to a Christmas tree when she was in high school. In that snapshot she looks as if something good is waiting for her under the tree. "Bennett is *perfectly* all right. It's the world around him that's out of line." Her voice had real punch, like Dad's does, when he's making a point.

"What if he stays gay?" I asked her.

"He'll still be Bennett, won't he?" she answered, and that's when she noticed the picture of Mickey Mantle on the back of the door. "That's new, isn't it?" she asked. I told her Valerie and Gretchen had given it to me, and Bennett had hung it. I was surprised she hadn't spotted it before this. She sort of tilted her head to give it a better once-over and I could see her wheels were turning. "I bet Mickey Mantle's mother was no more proud of her son than I am of mine," she said after a minute or two. "Straight or gay. You're both batting a thousand with me."

Dad didn't get back in half an hour. Not an hour later, either. When I went to bed, he still hadn't come home, and at first, I couldn't sleep. I think Bennett was wide awake too, pretending to be sacked out, but waiting to hear Dad's car, like I was. But by the time my father did come back, I was asleep and his voice woke me. "Bennett, Bennett, get up," Dad was whispering, probably trying not to make too much noise. It didn't work; I sat right up in bed like he'd yelled, *Fire.* "Not you, Matthew, you go back to sleep," Dad said.

"Where were you?" I asked. It was midnight, at least.

"I had to drive forty miles to find a hardware store open at this hour," Dad said, still whispering.

What was he talking about? Bennett was getting out of bed, rummaging around for his jeans. He'd thrown them over a chair and in the light that was coming in from the hall, I could see him pushing his feet into them. "Where are you going?" I asked. I was half in and out of a dream about a Ouija board that could forecast softball scores and hated to leave it. Right now I needed a happy dream.

"Go back to sleep," Bennett said.

"What's happening?" I asked. I was hard into reality by

this time, saw Dad in the doorway wearing a raincoat and waiting for my brother.

"Dad, it's raining," Bennett was saying. He'd looked out the window on his way to get his sneakers from under his desk. "You can't paint wet doors!"

That's when I got the flash. Dad had gone all over town looking for paint.

"I've got an umbrella, Bennett," Dad said. "And we're damn well going to try."

I stayed awake long enough to go to the window in Dad's office where I could see the front of the house. Although the rain was really splashing down, I could see the sack with the rat had disappeared and the lady's brassiere was gone from the basketball hoop. Right below the window, I saw Dad and my brother, with umbrellas in one hand and paintbrushes in the other. They were standing in puddles next to each other, smearing white paint over the six black letters on our garage door.

29

Valerie and Gretchen were standing on our doorstep the next morning, Saturday, both dressed in overalls and painter's hats. Dad invited them in and offered them coffee, but they said they had no time for coffee but thank you, some other time. They did come into the living room, though, which is how I happened to hear every word they said.

"We were on our way to take Blanche to the vet's last night. We didn't want her to get sick from the fumes when we were wallpapering and painting," Gretchen explained. "When we pulled up to the stop sign at the corner, some kids went by, and they were sort of like, *too loud.* You know, laughing and yelling. One threw something, I guess it was a spray can, and he tried to hit a mailbox with it. They weren't from this neighborhood, for sure. Then, on the way back, as we drove by your house, we saw this horrible—this word—painted on your garage door. We kept trying to call you."

Gretchen went on to say they were very upset to see what she thought of as a "message of hate." "Was this aimed at one of the boys?" she asked my parents. Mom had come downstairs and looked at Dad, who was shaking his head no. Bennett was still in bed and I was in the kitchen, eating a banana, fueling up for my softball game and edging toward the door, to get a better view of the action. The rain had stopped, the sky was blue, and things didn't seem as bad as they had last night. I didn't know the worst was yet to come.

"We're not absolutely sure it was aimed at one of our boys," Mom said, giving Dad an uneasy look. I had the feeling she was ready to talk about Bennett, but didn't want to upset Dad. "We don't really know for sure," she continued, which was basically true, from her point of view. Not from mine, of course, and not from Bennett's either.

"Did you call the police?" Gretchen asked. She said she and Valerie noticed that the garage door had been painted over this morning. "Painted over" was not exactly what I would have called it. "Smeared over" was more like it. The first thing I'd done when I woke up was take a look at the paint job, which was a smudgy hodgepodge of swirly gray splotches that looked like what anyone would call a holy mess.

"We're going to redo the garage door as soon as the paint dries a bit," Dad said right away, sounding like this was an apology, which it sort of was and wasn't, depending how you looked at it. "I know it's a mess, but we didn't think all the neighbors should have to look at that graffiti—"

Valerie was shifting from one foot to the other, as if she were impatient, and wanted to say something. On the other hand, it was Gretchen who was doing a lot of the talking. "You didn't call the police?" she asked again, but there was more to it. The look on her face said, *Why didn't you?*

Mom looked even more uncomfortable than Dad.

Now *she* offered coffee, and was politely turned down too. Valerie was now stepping up to the plate. "If you don't, we will," she said. She looked at Gretchen. "We think it's important to have this on record."

"Wait a minute—" Dad began explaining about how he didn't want to "draw attention" to what had happened, and preferred just to forget about it, but that got Valerie shaking her head.

Dad kept talking. "It's just a bunch of kids, a bit of spring fever, no one was hurt, we don't want to make a federal case of kids' mischief . . ." He never mentioned the rat, from my point of view a major federal case.

Gretchen had taken a step back out of the living room into the hall and was also looking like she disapproved of what Dad was saying. "Is this about Matthew?" she asked, and I nearly dropped my banana, but Dad quick shook his head and cleared that up. "No, not Matthew!" He gave a quirky laugh, like someone had told a joke that wasn't too funny but he wanted to be polite.

"It's about *Bennett*," Mom squared her shoulders, sort of came to attention like she was a soldier ready for a long march, and I have to give her credit. I knew Dad would blow his stack about this later, but she was ready to carry the banner and take the heat. "Bennett is gay," she said. It sounded like she was announcing some plain old fact, like "Bennett is getting a pair of new shoes," or another totally ordinary piece of news.

I saw Dad's face but knew he'd never hit a wall with company here. "Now, Lydia, that's not quite right. He just *thinks* he is," he quickly put in, and I could see this didn't sit that well with Gretchen.

"Maybe you ought to take Bennett's word for it," she said with a little cough, and Valerie shook her head in agreement. "He'd be the one to know, wouldn't he?"

"He's only fifteen," Dad said, but it was as if he'd whispered the words and no one heard him. Gretchen and Valerie said a polite good-bye and that was pretty much the end of their visit. As they walked out the door they told Dad *they'd* be calling the police, and a minute later, although she lowered her voice, I heard what Mom said when she saw them out.

"I wouldn't have told anyone about Bennett but you. I knew he'd have told you himself, and you'll respect his privacy, won't you?"

I didn't hear the answer to that question, but stepped out of the kitchen just in time to see Valerie put her arms around Mom, just like Mrs. DeWitt had. As soon as Dad spotted me, he told me to go upstairs and wake Bennett. "We have more painting to do," he said, and then I thought I heard him speak a word under his breath I'm not allowed to use. As I went upstairs to wake Bennett I was really glad to be me today, and not my brother.

Sure enough, two police cars pulled up at the curb in front of our house not five minutes later.

Bennett was up by then, and although he sat at the dining room table looking zinged, when the policeman asked if he had any idea who was responsible for the "damage to the property" he spoke up loud and clear. It must have been the midnight paint job in the rain that turned him from a clam into an informer. "I guess I know," he told them. "At least, I have a pretty good idea."

30

In a way, coming down with whatever bug the triplets had given me was not so bad. I was so busy coughing, sneezing, and shivering, that I didn't concentrate on the fever in the house. Wrapped up in about twenty blankets, I was lying in the den, watching cartoon show reruns when I wasn't sleeping or trying to swallow spoonfuls of the pink poison Mom calls medication.

She was at home to take care of me and to the best of my knowledge she and Dad and Bennett had hardly said a word about anything at all since the police left. I heard them eating in the kitchen, clinking glasses and clicking knives and forks, but it didn't seem many words were spoken except, "Please pass the maple syrup." or "More bacon?" This was Sunday, the day after the police—three cops, three cars—had stood around in our living room with clipboards, then looked at the garage door and taken "statements" from all of us. They asked about a million questions and looked very serious. I kept noticing the clubs and guns in their belts and imagining what they'd do to Go-go and the amigos once they put handcuffs on their wrists and led them off. It made me feel better to know they might lock them up right next to murderers and thieves in a maximum security prison, obviously where they belonged. I think it was the flu giving me imaginitis; unfortunately, that's not what happened at all.

For one thing, Valerie and Gretchen had not seen the perps and neither had anyone else. We were sure we knew who'd be capable of throwing dead rats and painting low-blow messages on garage doors, but there were no fingerprints or tire marks. We could only give the police hints, which didn't translate into handcuffs.

Then, Saturday night, the doorbell rang. I was in a flu haze, but I do remember Dad opening the door and then slamming it shut and telling Mom not to open the door to any other reporters. They were "out there" and "swarming" and so were photographers taking pictures of our house. I could see the flashes right through the curtains. Bennett was told not to talk to ANYBODY. My brother talking to any living soul about what happened at our house was a very long shot.

The Monday afternoon paper had a picture of our house at the top of the second page.

LOCAL FAMILY VICTIMS OF HATE CRIME

was the headline. Mom forgot she'd put the thermometer in my mouth while she was reading the article under it and later Bennett said something like, "It's not the 'victims.' It's 'victim.' The grammar is wrong. And the sense is wrong too! It's only me. It should have nothing to do with the family! They got the headline all wrong!"

We got on the evening TV news too. A picture of our house flashed on the screen and a lady said, "Police are investigating this latest hate crime."

Bennett wouldn't sit down to dinner that night, but went right to Dad's office to use the computer. He said he was going to write a letter to the newspaper, but I don't think he ever did, because just as he went running upstairs, the telephone rang. Dad told Mom not to pick it up; "It's probably another reporter, Lydia." She was in the den with me and had two pills in the palm of her hand, and of course I figured she was heading my way, but instead, she just put them in her own mouth and swallowed them without even a glass of water.

I'm not sure what played out the rest of that evening, but I do know that at that minute it wasn't a reporter calling. It was Mr. DeWitt. I didn't know what it was he said exactly, and as I mentioned, I was pretty much blotto what with all the germs in my head fighting off the pink stuff and vice versa, but I know that Dad's voice sounded like two crooks spliced together. "I understand" and "If that's how you feel!" is all I heard, though I think there was a lot more said. My father was marching around the dining room with the phone, and when I got up to go to the bathroom I saw Mom was in the doorway, watching. She had a glass of water in her hand by this time, and was sort of leaning against the door frame. I remember thinking she looked sicker than I felt. At one point I thought it was all a virus dream.

As soon as Dad ended the telephone conversation, he went into the kitchen and closed the door to have a private conversation with Mom. It was a bunch of whispers, which always means *something* of industrial-strength going on, and if I'd felt better, I'd have tried to eavesdrop, but now my eyes were drooping shut and I had no choice in the matter. I let them.

Next thing I knew I was up in my own bed, alone with

the moon and the picture of Mickey Mantle on the back of the door, and I was dying of thirst.

"Bennett!" I whispered, hoping he was in his bed and awake, and would go to the bathroom and get me a glass of water, or better yet, go down to the kitchen and bring me some cream soda on ice. "Bennett?"

No answer, no Bennett. Where was he? And what time was it, anyway? I dragged myself out of bed and was heading for the bathroom when I heard Mom and Dad in the kitchen. No whispers this time. Arguing. Their voices went loud, then soft, then loud. It was as if they remembered they had to keep it down because it was late and they didn't want to wake me, but then there were words that jumped out of them like horn blasts when they got carried away.

"I'm not going to say it again, Lydia!"

"I heard you the first time!"

"They don't need to—"

"I'm not making this call."

"I didn't say you had to. Did I say you had to? I'm going to!"

"What are you going to say? Just tell me—"

"I'll find something to say, Lydia. Trust me."

"You're going to make up some story. What sort of story—?"

I realized, as I stood there in a blur, that Bennett was sitting in my spot, on my fourth step, taking it all in.

"What are they arguing about, Bennett?" I whispered.

At first, he didn't answer. I thought he hadn't heard me.

"What are they *fighting* about?"

Just my brother's not saying anything was saying a lot. "They're arguing about graduation. Dad doesn't want Grandma and Grandpa to come."

"He doesn't? Why doesn't he?"

"Why do you think, Matthew? Don't you *get* it? Why do you *think*? He doesn't want them to know about *me*!"

31

If I was shaking and weak in the knees, this time it wasn't the flu. I didn't know what was about to happen, but I was on a very thin edge. Bennett was now thumping down each step, flying in his bedroom slippers as if the stairs were on fire. When the fighting between Mom and Dad stopped cold I knew he'd arrived in the kitchen. I followed, feeling better but taking it slow, practically holding my breath. In a way, I was in no hurry to get into the middle of things; on the other hand, I didn't want to miss anything. Also, by this time I wanted that glass of cream soda pretty desperately.

When I got to the kitchen, Dad was standing at the coffeemaker pouring coffee into a mug. Mom was rummaging through a drawer, looking for something or other. Bennett was standing behind a kitchen chair, holding the back of it, sort of leaning against it. It was as if it were a railing holding him back from an eighty-foot drop off a cliff. Everyone was frozen in place, three wax museum statues with faces that looked like they'd come out of molds and would never, ever change.

But at least the fighting was on hold.

I coughed. "Matthew!" Mom was the first to spot me. "Where are your slippers!" A major crisis and she was worried about bare feet. That's my mother for you.

"My feet aren't cold, I'm just thirsty." I went to the cupboard for a glass. In a shot, Mom was next to me, her hand on my forehead. "The fever seems to have broken," she said.

"What's going on?" I asked, scared of the silence. I could actually hear the sound the refrigerator makes, which is practically no sound at all.

"You'd better go back to bed," Mom said. "It's got nothing to do with you, dear."

"Yes, it does!" Bennett burst out. "It does! Did you hear about Jeremy's dad, Matthew? Did you hear what he's *decreed*?" My brother was leaning against that chair looking as if it gave way, he'd be a dead duck.

"Decreed?" I wasn't sure what that meant. It sounded like a lesson in history, part of some serious royal document.

"I guess, I think—" For a moment I was confused. Wasn't this about Grandpa and Grandma? No, it wasn't and yes, I had heard that conversation earlier. It was not imaginitis.

Do you know what he *said*, Matthew?"

Out of the corner of my eye I saw Dad pour milk into his mug. I saw he was shaking his head, left to right, right to left, as if there were a mosquito buzzing around it and he was wanting to shake it off.

"Maybe this isn't the right time to discuss it, Bennett." Mom was back at the kitchen drawer, rummaging, rummaging. The way she was going at it made me think that maybe it was just something for her to do. Mom always seems to be moving, busy doing stuff, especially when there's stress.

"Matthew's gonna find out tomorrow anyhow, isn't he?" Bennett asked, without addressing anyone in particular.

"Tomorrow?" I coughed. Maybe the fever was back. Tomorrow? Find out *what*?

"Let him go back to bed—" Mom said to Bennett. "He's *sick*. He should be lying down. Where are your *slippers*?" she asked me again.

Bennett kept at it, full steam ahead like she hadn't said a word. "Maybe not tomorrow. Maybe day after tomorrow. Maybe Wednesday. Sooner or later he has to be told what Mr. DeWitt had to say. Why not *now*?"

I was beginning to gulp down the cream soda, which tasted good but was hurting my throat. I should've picked something without bubbles. "What did he say?" I asked.

"Tell him, Dad."

"You know what, Bennett? Maybe you should tell him."

"Actually, if you want to know, I don't give a *damn* what Mr. DeWitt said, but Matthew ought to hear it." Bennett was speaking in a high-test voice and ordinarily this would have resulted in a wall-slap, but not tonight. Dad was sipping his coffee, staying cool, his face still in his wax expression.

"You know something? It's not even a big deal. I don't even *care*," Bennett continued, and I don't remember ever seeing him stand up to Dad like this.

Dad surprised me too. His voice was sort of pleading. "I don't like the man very much, but look here, son . . ."

"HEY!" Bennett cut him off. "Listen, Matthew, guess what? Jeremy is not allowed to come over here anymore. And you probably won't be seeing much of Nolan, either."

"Not allowed? Here?" I never expect the unexpected, and this really came from out of left field.

"I'm contagious, see? Mr. DeWitt thinks what I've got is *catching*. And I don't mean a *virus*." Bennett coughed a couple of times then, which cut dead his hopped-up speech.

"Are *you* coming down with the flu now?" Mom sounded the way she sounds after she's worked a whole weekend, sort of out of gas.

I guess Bennett's answer was another cough, and then, "It's the rainbow kite. He will not allow any of his kids to be a part of it."

"WHAT?" I gulped down the last of my soda. "Why?" sailed out on a loud burp. I excused myself but I'm my brother's brother, after all. "WHY?"

"It's a fag thing, a rainbow kite. That's what he said, isn't it, Dad?"

Dad looked apologetic, well, almost. He didn't answer.

"Isn't it, Dad?" Bennett persisted. "He said it was a 'fag flag.' That's what you told me, Dad."

"Well, he's right about the rainbow. It's a *symbol*. For homosexuals. It's the gay flag. Isn't that right, Bennett? I mean, he was right on the money about *that*."

"The rainbow is a symbol?" I asked. "You mean when we see it in the sky too? I had never actually seen a real one, as I've said. Bennett had seen two, one right in the sky over our street.

"NO," Bennett was acting like I'd asked the dumbo question of the year. "Not in the *sky*, for crying out loud."

"I thought you meant, God had put it there as a sign for gay people—" I think I was sounding even more dodo, the way my brother's eyes rolled under his eyebrows.

"Matthew—are you KIDDING?"

But Mom smiled a little smile. "Maybe yes. Who knows what God intended?" she said.

At that point, Dad's eyes popped out. His cool was gone. His voice went *boom*. "Oh, for heaven's sake, Lydia, what are you *saying*?"

"I'll tell you what I'm saying!" Mom had pulled a pair of kitchen scissors out of the drawer—probably what she'd been looking for all along—and pointed them at Dad. Her voice went up and up too. "I'm saying God is not a homophobe! That's what I'm saying!"

Dad's eyes had red rings by this time, and he was aiming his mug at Mom. "And you're implying I am!"

Before I could ask what a homophobe was Bennett slammed the chair on the floor, hard, like he intended to break the legs right off it. I think he just meant to get everyone's attention but the sound was like an earthquake. "Don't fight! DON'T FIGHT! I'm not worth it!" he yelled at the top of his lungs, and when Mom and Dad stared, looking like they'd been turned back into wax on the spot, he lowered the pitch and let go of the chair. He looked like he was going to burst out in tears, but didn't. "You know what! I think everyone else would be better off if I were dead!" he cried, and he ran out of the kitchen before anyone could think of a word to say.

* * *

It was much later that I heard it. I was back in bed and half asleep, but I know I was not in the middle of a dream. It was high fidelity and went right through me, although at first I thought it was someone on TV taking a beating. But it wasn't, and it wasn't my brother, either; he was in the bunk bed above me and I guess he must have heard it too. It was coming from my parents' bedroom, right through the closed door, and it was a sound that tore me apart. It was my father, crying.

32

A homophobe is a person who hates gay people, I found out the next day. Mom explained it to me when she was shortening a pair of Bennett's pants she wanted me to wear to his graduation, which was only two weeks away. She was using the same scissors she'd pulled out of the kitchen drawer last night, which brought it all back full force, the all-out family war and what followed. I could hear Dad's crying again like it was happening this minute, which of course, it wasn't. He'd left earlier for Saint Louis; I heard him say good-bye to Mom, and I heard something else too. I was just coming out of the bathroom when he stopped at the door of our room.

Dad told Bennett that he didn't want him flying his kite at graduation. "Believe me, son, it's not in your best interests," he said, after he'd asked my brother how he was feeling. Then, in a voice so low I could hardly hear it, he added, "Get rid of it, Bennett. Get rid of the damn thing!"

I stood still for a minute, waiting to hear what my brother's reaction would be, expecting maybe an ear-splitting scream or other earthshaking sound effects, but all I heard was a bunch of coughs, a sneeze, and then Dad's footsteps like an echo as he walked back down the stairs.

Mom had me standing on a kitchen chair, and I was

looking at the top of her head when I asked her if she thought Dad was a homophobe. For some reason it was easier to ask her when she wasn't looking into my face, and I wasn't looking into hers.

She had to take pins out of her mouth to answer.

"He's trying very hard not to be," she said, which isn't what I wanted to hear. Maybe that's why I didn't want Mom to see my face, which probably had disappointment written all over it. I wanted a flat-out NO. Go-go and the amigos were homophobes, not my father! And what if it turned out I was gay too? When I didn't answer right away, Mom must have given it more thought, because she added, "The most important thing is that he's trying to protect Bennett," and that sounded a lot better.

Then, while I was still high on the kitchen chair with one pants cuff pinned up and the other one still hanging over my shoe, the telephone rang. "Don't move, Matthew," Mom said when she went to answer it. She'd misplaced the phone again, and had to leave the kitchen to go into the hall, where she'd left it under some stuff she meant to take to the dry cleaner's.

I could tell she was speaking to Grandma, but what with the TV blaring in the den I didn't hear what she was saying. With me still elevated, Mom cut the conversation pretty short, and when she came back to the kitchen, she told me now both Grandma's knees were giving her a lot of trouble. She and Grandpa wouldn't be coming to Bennett's graduation after all.

What Mom didn't say is what I figured out right away. One problem was solved; Dad wouldn't have to make up a story to keep my grandparents from coming here. And while Grandma and Grandpa would miss graduation and my brother and I would miss *them*, they'd be kept in the dark about rainbows, hate crimes, and the truth about their grandson.

My brother was covered to his chin in blankets on the den couch now, and it was his turn to be bleary-eyed and to swallow disgusting pink meds, watch reruns and get special attention. The difference was that I'd sort of enjoyed being home with the flu, but Bennett looked flat-out miserable. He wouldn't talk to me at all, saying his throat hurt, and more than anything it was the rainbow kite; after all this time and all this work, Dad's ruling—*his* decree—not to fly the kite at graduation, was scary I guess for my brother, flying the kite at graduation was *everything*.

I know my brother pretty well. That's why I think for him, giving up the kite was like going off the cliff he'd been on the edge of since Frankie died. Which sort of explains the unexplainable: what happened later that night. When we were both in our pajamas and ready for bed, Bennett started looking for something in his closet. "What are you doing? You're sick. You're supposed to be in bed," I reminded him. He was pulling stuff out from under other stuff, making a big mess in the middle of the floor, and then, he finally found it: his dog and cat stamp collection. He was shivering, although the room wasn't a bit cold. "You keep this," he said, handing me the Christmas box. Then he gave me the blue metal bank he keeps his money in. "The combination is 6, 26, 22. Keep that too. I want you to have it."

"What are you giving all this stuff to me for, Bennett?" I asked. I thought either the germs or the meds had affected his mind.

"I told you I couldn't talk, didn't I?" my brother said in a raspy whisper, pointing to his throat. "Just keep the stuff. I won't be needing any of it anymore."

"You won't? Why not?" I wanted to know.

Bennett shook his head, climbed up into his bed, and told me to turn off the light. I did what he told me to, but I couldn't fall asleep, not for a long, long time.

33

My brother was drinking honey and lemon tea, eating a muffin and saying nothing in the kitchen when I left for school the next day. I didn't take the bus; Mom drove me on her way to Mrs. Dowd's. She said she'd come back at lunch to check in on Bennett, who was feeling better, but still coughing. She also reminded me to practice the saxophone, not give away the apple she'd put in my lunch bag, and not forget to take another spoonful of the pink stuff when I got home. Although I'd recovered, I had to finish what was left in the bottle. I told Mom the medicine tasted like toxic waste. When she laughed, I realized I hadn't heard my mother laugh in a very long time.

So I left in sort of an upbeat mood, not knowing the rest of the day would turn out surreal.

I can't explain the unexplainable, but two weird things happened to me at school. The first took place in Algebra class, when Kim Yee handed me an invitation to her birthday party. "I was going to mail it. See? I already put a stamp on the envelope," she whispered when Mr. Gold was at the blackboard with his back turned to the class. "Were you very sick?" she wanted to know.

Then she said, "I can help you catch up if you want me to," and she gave me this sort of wink with one of her eyes. I said, "Okay," and she said, "Well, *okay*," and she smiled at me in a cool, airy way. That's when I guess a little beam of light went right into me, as if she'd touched me with a wand with a magic sparkle tip, or something. I decided she was cute. Her hair was really nice, and she had very straight white teeth. I realized her braces had just been replaced with the almost-invisible kind and she had a new eyebrow ring. So it just hit me: I liked her in a way I'd never liked her before. It was actually like a little blastoff; knowing that second, right in the middle of Algebra class, with Mr. Gold telling us to turn to page 68 in the workbook, that I was not likely to be gay.

Later that day, as I was sitting in computer class, I remembered the birthday party invitation, which I'd stuck in my notebook. When I looked at it again, something altogether different switched on in my head. It was the stamp Kim had put on it, a picture of an eagle, not a dog, but still, it reminded me of my brother's stamp collection. I thought: it's not my brother's anymore, now it's mine, and just as I had that thought, the screen of the monitor in front of me went suddenly dark. Had I touched a wrong key? I hadn't. But now all I saw was a message written across the glass in block letters: GO HOME NOW.

I'd just had lunch in the cafeteria and seen Go-go Mallis sitting across the room with his amigos as if nothing whatsoever had gone wrong to throw a curve into *his* life. His suspension was over; there he was, about to blow a paper from his drinking straw into the air with his buddies having a great old time all around him. Where were the handcuffs? Where was Justice?

Somebody had said the police had questioned him and

a few of the amigos. Everybody had denied everything.

Jeremy came over to ask how Bennett was feeling and to tell me Nolan—actually all three triplets—were down with the flu and he himself wasn't feeling any too good. He didn't stay to eat his sandwich with me.

"Is it true you won't be coming to our house anymore?" I asked him before he moved off, and he shrugged. I guess he was too embarrassed to answer. He didn't have to; watching him walk away was answer enough.

When I saw the GO HOME NOW message on the computer screen I blinked a couple of times, closed my eyes, and when I opened them again, the message was gone. I told myself I'd imagined it, but right then and there, I got up from my seat, walked to the front of the classroom, told Mr. Manheim that this was an emergency, and before he could say a word, ran out of the room. I think someone stopped to ask if I had a hall pass, but I just kept going as if my feet were atom-driven. I know it took me a long time because the school bus wasn't operating and I didn't have my bike, but I ran most of the way, and I couldn't tell you why. I just had a *feeling*, a strong sense that the message I'd read on the computer monitor was major league business and that even if I'd imagined it, I dared not ignore it.

As it was, I made it just in time.

34

At first, walking through the door, I didn't get the idea that anything in the house was out of order. I didn't expect to open the door and find a man-eating serpent in the kitchen or a bonfire in the living room, but I sensed something definitely different the minute I walked through the door. The thing was, the house was totally and absolutely silent. Usually, there's the TV, or there's music, or the telephone ringing, or at least, especially with Bennett being sick, a cough or two. Not a sound. All that pin-drop stillness was giving me the jitters.

I called up the stairs. "Bennett?" and again, "Bennett?" and got no answer. For a pretty good reason, I didn't think he would be asleep upstairs. The thing is, when we're sick, we like to be sick in front of the TV, and near the kitchen. That's where Bennett would likely have fallen asleep. Sure enough, his blanket was heaped on the couch in the den, but my brother was not under it. I called his name again, and when I got no answer, checked the kitchen. There was a half-eaten sandwich and an empty cup with a tea bag hanging out of it, but no Bennett.

I began climbing the stairs. I didn't take the steps two at a time, the way anyone would; to tell the truth, by this time I was pretty spooked. I felt like I was creeping along through a horror film, that any minute a trapdoor might open, or some unexpected *thing* would jump out of the shadows, throwing its cold hands around my neck.

Only there were no shadows, it was broad daylight, and there was no hint of a break-in. "Bennett?" I called again. The bathroom door was open—no one there—and no one was in my parents' bedroom, either. The door to Bennett's and my room was closed, and believe it or not, I had to take a deep breath, pull in extra oxygen, just to turn the doorknob. "Bennett?" I said, pushing the door open very slowly.

But the room was empty. *Empty?* How could that be? My brother was supposed to be home sick with the flu. Then, I practically laughed out loud with relief. Here I was, seeing messages on a computer screen, expecting to meet doom face to face in the middle of the afternoon, acting out some kind of spine-tingler fantasy when where Bennett was was suddenly very obvious. Mom must have checked him out at lunch and decided to take him to the doctor's. They'd probably walk in any minute, wanting to know why the heck I was home too early from school.

Just then, the telephone rang and I practically jumped a foot. In all the quiet, a little ring sounded like a cannon shot. When I pulled myself together and was turning to leave the room to answer it, I saw a white sheet of paper lying on Bennett's desk. It was new; I was pretty sure I hadn't seen it this morning, not that I was absolutely sure. I don't notice much during my usual rush to get dressed in time to get to school. Anyway, I picked it up and headed out but didn't make it by the second ring, which is when the answering machine picked up.

When I heard Mom's voice, I froze.

"Bennett," she was saying, "pick up, dear. Bennett? Are you asleep? Bennett? Bennett!"

I raced down the stairs and grabbed the telephone before she could hang up. "Mom. It's me. It's Matthew. Isn't Bennett with you—?"

"—Matthew? What are you doing at home? It's only—what do you mean, is Bennett with me? He's home with the flu! I left him there an hour and a half ago!"

"He's not here, Mom," I said.

"Of course he's there. Did you check your room?"

"I did!" I looked down at the white paper I'd picked up off his desk and got a top-to-bottom chill. He'd decorated it with fat, black lines going around the page, like a picture frame. His name was written out in large, bold type at the top. Arial Black. I recognized his favorite font.

"What about the garage? He's probably down there, puttering around with his kite!"

Of course, I'd never thought of that. I said I'd run down and check, and Mom said she'd hold.

I was pretty sure I wouldn't find my brother in the garage and I was right. Everything tidy, the ping pong table litter-free. And not a sign of Bennett.

What I didn't expect was that the rainbow kite would be gone too.

35

Bennett Lawson Cummings,
born November 6, 1986,
student at Clara Barton Junior High School,
class of 2001,
son of Alexander and Lydia Cummings.
Died on May 24th at age 15.
He leaves behind a brother, Matthew,
grandparents Nellie and Arthur Eldridge
of Minneapolis,Minnesota.
Cause of death: SHAME

"Come home, Mom!" I yelled into the phone. My heart was jumping so hard I could practically feel it against my shirt.

I didn't say a word to my mother about Bennett's obituary, which he must have created and printed out some time today. I was afraid if I read it to her, her heart might begin acting up like mine was, and at her age, who knew but that it could stop dead in its tracks. Today was May 24.

I slammed down the telephone and picked it back up to call 911. Then I thought better of it. What if he'd just been goofing around, having gotten tired of watching reruns or playing video games? It's not like I'd found a gun missing or an empty bottle of poison lying around in the bathroom. On the other hand . . .what *if*?

WHAT IF? Just as I'd seen the letters spelling GO HOME NOW clear as anything in front of my eyes, I got another message from what must be the same back compartment in my head. I took Bennett's death notice with me so Mom wouldn't find it and left her a note: "Going to find Bennett. Be home soon," and I put it on the kitchen table where she couldn't miss it. At marathon speed, I headed for my bike, and it wasn't until I'd pedaled down the street and was past Gretchen and Valerie's house that I remembered what I'd forgotten. Never mind; I'd take a spoon of the terrible pink stuff later.

I've never really put my bike to the test and I have to give it credit. It was as if when I needed to fly, it grew wings on its wheels. Of course it didn't leave the ground, but at one point, when I was past Knickerbocker Avenue, had gone through downtown, and was turning the corner—against the light!—of Waterview Road, it seemed to lift off the pavement and spin its wheels in the air. I think I was coughing a lot all the way there, but it's mind over matter, as Mr. Gold always says, and my mind was going all cylinders, forgetting matter.

Funny thing, all the way out to Edgewater Point, memories of stuff Bennett had done for me were clicking in: things I hadn't thought about for like a hundred years. Once, Bennett found a five-dollar bill on the street. He saw it and I didn't, but he bought me a book of prehistoric animals stickers, spent half the money on me, saying we were together when he found it and I deserved half. And knowing how I don't like green peas, he'd always make them disappear off my plate so I wouldn't get heat for not eating any. Pedaling along like crazy, I remembered now, of all things, the books he used to read to me before I knew how to, even when I asked him to read them over and over and *over*. Then, Bennett taught me how to tie fancy knots with rope—I'd almost forgotten that!—and let me use his camera when my class went on a field trip. When I dropped it and broke the lens, he didn't even get that mad.

He pumped up my bike tire and watered the lawn for me when it was my turn and showed me how to pick up little meteorites using a magnet at the beach. Thanks to Bennett, that experiment got me a lot of attention from Mr. Gold, and really helped pull up my grade. He taught me to whistle too!

And of course he saved me from being zapped the day my kite flew into the power line. Maybe even risked his own life!

All these things came back to me for reasons I can't explain. It was like I was having a life rerun, which got me coughing and crying and talking to God and to Bennett and the moon, begging them all—while I was pedaling with all my strength—to please, *please* stop everything and save my brother.

36

It was the worst sight I'd ever seen in my life: Bennett's rainbow kite suspended in the blue sky over Edgewater Point.

I stopped my bike and tried to breathe normally, but the sight knocked the wind right out of me. The kite was bobbing along, being carried out to sea by the wind, getting smaller and smaller even as I had my eyes glued to it, as if I could will it to stop dead right there in the sky—*Stopstopstop!* It was suspended in space, and I guess the line had turned invisible in the blue air. What made it so terrible to see, what shot me down as I stood there trying to catch my breath, was that Bennett wasn't there, the spool tight in his hand, holding and guiding it. The kite had escaped—or worse—he'd let it go, sent it to wherever, to the end of the earth, to nowhere, to oblivion, to the *moon*, because he'd just buckled under. Written his death notice, and given up. What else was there to think? He'd let go the kite, bailed out on living. What else could it mean?

I thought back to the day we'd put Frankie in his cardboard box coffin and let him slip over the side of the fishing bridge, to which I was just now running, with what little breath I had left. I'd dropped my bike and just sprinted forward across the dunes. I had so many tears running out of my eyes I would have said the bridge was underwater—and I was sure so was my brother. Two men were heading toward it from the tackle shop and I couldn't help but glance at the row of gulls on the roof and wonder if these birds were the same ones that had watched Frankie's funeral. Had they seen my brother jump too? The fishermen had arrived with their gear and were moving closer. I heard them laughing as I was running. *Laughing!* How could anyone anywhere in the world be having fun at a time when everything in the universe seemed to have quit cold, wrapped up, *ended*?

One of them had spotted the kite, was pointing at it, and now both stopped to stare up at it. I don't know why, but I wanted to stop them. *It's my brother's rainbow kite and it's private!* I wanted to yell out, but instead I just ran onto the bridge and leaned over the railing and looked down at the water. That is, I tried looking down *into* it, *past* it, right through all the salty wetness in my own eyes. I tried to *search* it. I ran up and down the length of the bridge, peering down, trying to see under the surface, which seemed just as dense as dark syrup, as if someone had poured buckets of black molasses right into the water. I thought maybe Bennett was trapped down under the bridge, already drowned. Or maybe he'd floated out to sea—or possibly the fish had gotten him and there was nothing at all of him left. I was bawling hard now. *My brother, my brother, my brother!* Panic kept cramming up my throat. Drowned! Gone!

I had the idea of diving in, then, just jumping off the bridge and maybe, maybe, if he was somewhere down there and there was still a drop of life in him, pulling him out, giving him mouth-to-mouth, saving him.

But the men had walked onto the bridge and were coming closer. They kept talking and laughing as they came near, and then one of them noticed me. "Hey," he called out. "Hey, kid? What happened? You okay?" I sort of shook my head yes, wanting them to be gone, but they were standing there, looking at me.

The other man said, "Is that your kite up there?" and I didn't answer. They guessed I was upset because it had got away. I let them think whatever they wanted to think.

"Too bad. Nice kite," the first man said. "Great colors. Pretty big too. Shame you lost it."

"I guess it's another big one that got away." They both laughed at that and then the first man said, "Don't feel bad, son. You'll get another one. It's only a kite, after all."

That's when I ran off the bridge, pounded across the dunes to my bike, and headed home to break the news to my mother.

37

I almost didn't make it home. I practically rear-ended a van that had stopped for a red light. "Watch out!" someone on the sidewalk screamed and I braked, just in time. Twice I had to stop because my throat clogged up, maybe with crying or coughing or fear, and once I stopped, pulled off the road, just to try to figure out how I could say what I had to say to Mom.

By the time I pulled into our driveway, I felt really sick. The flu was back full force, and worse. There was Mom's car looking dusty as usual, with the little dent in the fender where she'd backed into a fire hydrant, and I thought about how many places it had driven me and Bennett and how now there would always be an empty space in the back seat next to me. I didn't want to go into the house; I wanted just to turn back time, have it be this morning or last night, when I was under my covers in my bed and Bennett was lying in his bunk right above me. I stood there a minute, not wanting to put away my bike or go to the door, when unexpectedly it flew open.

Mom stood on the doorstep. "Matthew! For God's sake!" she said. Her voice was crackling fire, like someone had put a match to it. "Where have you been? And without your bike helmet! Put your bike away and come in this minute!"

I put my bike in the garage the way I always do, and

there was Shearon's dolly leaning against the wall. I didn't even ask myself how Bennett managed to get the kite up to Edgewater Point without it, but went up the stairs to the kitchen. Mom was waiting there for me, her eyes and nose a terrible pink. She had a tissue in her hand and was blowing her nose; maybe she already knew. She was shaking her head, and told me Dad would be back tonight because she'd called him in Saint Louis, asked him to come home right away. "You didn't take your medicine, did you?" she said as if that mattered now, and then went plop down in a kitchen chair as if she couldn't stand on her feet even a minute longer.

She put her hands up to her face, sort of holding up her head. She closed her eyes and got quiet, while I got in another chair, shaking head to foot. There was a terrible long spell of silent nothing, where everything stopped and I could hear my pulse beating in both ears. "Something horrible happened, Matthew."

I started to say I know, *I know*, but she went on, "Your brother almost died today."

Had I heard this right? *Almost*?

"He almost drowned."

I opened my mouth and nothing came out except another cough. Suddenly my mother went from what I thought was misery into blowing a fuse, just like that.

"And you! Taking off like that! You've just gotten over the flu, for heaven's sakes! And now I think you've got a fever again!" Her hand went to my forehead like it was on autopilot, and the way I felt, I was surprised her fingers didn't get a third-degree burn. "You didn't take your medicine either Matthew, did you? *Did you?*" Then she got up, no kidding, to find the bottle of pink stuff and the spoon to go with it.

I was still speechless, but now I managed to croak out one word: "Bennett—"

"He went to Edgewater Point, sick as he was! What's wrong with you boys? Do you think you're *immortal*? Your brother gets out of his sickbed to go to the shore to send his kite off on some kind of farewell voyage—I blame your father for some of this!—and tries to videotape the thing flying off into the sky or to Australia or something, and then—then— " She had to stop to blow her nose and let a tear squeeze out of one of her eyes before she went on, "and then, he fell over the railing of the bridge. He—luckily, your brother is a strong swimmer, or, or, or . . ."

Mom stopped to pull back weeps and to wipe her eyes and to swallow hard a couple of times but finally, she got it all out, how Bennett dragged himself onto the shore and someone at the tackle shop saw him and took him inside and wrapped him in some rags and plastic bags and the owner drove him—and the video camera and Shearon's dolly—home. "If they hadn't spotted him, what would have happened I don't know—" she began, before stopping to blow her nose again.

She pushed the bottle of pink meds and the spoon in front of me and waited for me to take some.

"Where is Bennett now?" I asked, after I'd swallowed it obediently and quickly down. This time, I hardly tasted the terrible stuff.

Mom pointed to the ceiling, meaning upstairs, in our room. He was in bed, I guessed. "He doesn't have pneumonia. His lungs are clear and that's a miracle. But he's running a high fever and he's a very sick boy. And Matthew, he's totally lost his voice."

"You mean, he can't talk?" I asked Mom.

"He can't talk," she said, and then, beaming in on some spot over my shoulder instead of looking into my eyes the way she usually does, she added, "or, he just . . . won't."

38

If the worst sight I'd ever seen in my life was the rainbow kite slowly disappearing into nothing in the sky, the best sight ever was my brother sacked out and not dead, just dead to the world, in my bed. I stood practically on top of him for a few seconds to make sure he was breathing, and then I said, "I love you, mucho-mucho," in a bird voice. Blanche's words just popped out of me without my planning it. If Bennett had heard it, it would have been like the most embarrassing moment in my life. Of course, I said it so quietly no one could possibly have picked it up without radar. Later, I even imagined I'd only thought I'd said it, but either way, the feeling came over me, and if my brother hadn't been so sick, I might even have jumped on top of him and thrown my arms around his whole body to make sure he was real.

I tried to tell myself it was the flu bug making me act crazy, talk like a cockatoo, but the truth is, when I said "I love you," whether it came out of my mouth or didn't, I meant all the words. It washed over me, and sick as I was, I crawled up on Bennett's bunk so relieved I went to sleep smiling and slept without even dreaming until the next morning.

I woke up coughing and Mom came in to tell me no one in the family would be going to school—or anywhere—today. Bennett was still asleep and one would have thought it was a very old man, not a kid, lying there in the bottom bunk; with his head half under the covers he was making loud Grandpa snoring sounds. "It's bronchial involvement," Mom whispered, and said she was going to the drugstore to pick up stronger medication the doctor had called in earlier.

Mom stuck a thermometer in my mouth and I came out with not exactly flying colors—"Still sick! See what happens when you push your luck?"—and she followed that with a whispered lecture about taking risks, recovery from illness, and wearing bike helmets. I sort of listened, trying hard to look serious, but another day off from school, Bennett here and alive, and Dad home for the day all added up to a big bonanza for me. It was all I could do not to LOL and dance up a storm of happiness around my room.

But then Bennett woke up and I remembered I still had his death notice stuck in the pocket of my baseball jacket. My brother was awake but bleary-eyed. Not really sitting up, not lying down either, but sort of in-between. He had a spot of red on each cheek like a circus clown and the whites of his eyes were half closed and pink too. My pillow was sort of behind his neck, keeping his head from flopping back down. I leaned over the side of the top bunk and asked him, "Did you really *fall* in, Bennett?" and at first he acted like he hadn't heard the question, until I asked him again.

"Did you actually *fall* over the railing of the bridge?" I sort of knew the answer because you'd have to climb the rail before you could fall over it; it's that high. Diving off that bridge is forbidden any time of year. So they had made the barrier extra high to be sure kids wouldn't be tempted.

Bennett shook his head no.

"You jumped, didn't you?" I asked. I wanted my brother to tell me somebody had pushed him, or he'd climbed up just to get a better shot taking the video of the kite; I wanted him to tell me anything except what I knew was the truth.

My brother nodded his head yes. His mouth moved and said "I jumped," but no sound came out.

"I knew it," I said. "I found the thing you wrote and left on your desk."

My brother got out of bed then, sort of heaved himself off the mattress and took about five wobbly steps over to his desk. He began rummaging through the top drawer and finally found what he was looking for, his pen with the flashlight tip. He tore a piece of paper from a notebook lying on top of the desk, wobbled his way back to bed, sat on the edge, and started writing.

"What are you doing?" I asked, but realized he was writing me a note. When he finished, he held it out so I could lean over the side and grab it to read.

I JUMPED BUT DON'T TELL MOM OR DAD I MENT TO SWIM OUT BUT I GOT SCARED AND SWUM BACK IN. DON'T TELL MOM OR DAD PROMISE

Bennett never makes spelling or grammar mistakes so I knew he was pretty sick. He suddenly remembered something else and waved for me to give him back the paper. Then, he scribbled some more.

WHERE IS THE OBITUARY?

"I still have it," I told him.

GIVE IT BACK, he wrote.

"Bennett promise you'll never try to jump again!"

My brother shook his head no.

YOU DON'T KNOW WHAT ITS LIKE

"If you died you would've killed Mom too. Maybe even Dad," I said. *"Didn't you think of that?"*

He stopped writing and sort of sagged forward. The way he was shivering I was afraid he was going to fall over and hit the floor.

"Bennett, promise, you won't try it again or I'll give the note to Dad," I threatened.

I could see his pen was shaking and he took a long time with it.

I'D BE BETTER OFF BEING DEAD

"No, you wouldn't! You wouldn't!" I cried. I started to cough and couldn't stop.

I'M ALWAYS HIDING WHO I AM

Bennett scribbled. At first it was hard to read, some letters jerky or too close to each other and some i's without dots. I looked down over his shoulder, coughing.

I HATE ME I HATE ME I HATE ME

I climbed down from my brother's bunk, barking coughs. I needed a drink of water.

AND SO DOES EVERYONE ELSE

"Not me! Not Mom, not Dad or Grandma or Grandpa," I reminded my brother when I could get my own voice working.

THEY'RE BETTER OFF WITHOUT ME

"No, they're not! *We're* not!" I felt hot, then cold, then

dizzy trying to think. What I finally came up with was, "How would you feel if it was me that drowned? How would you feel, Bennett?"

Maybe that did it. Maybe not. I went to the bathroom for a drink of water and when I came back, I pulled the death notice out of the pocket of my baseball jacket. While I held it over his head my brother swore on the memory of Frankie, in wobbly writing, he'd absolutely never try anything like that again.

39

Dad came into our room a little while later. He was carrying a tray with toast and tea on it, and he pulled up a chair, sat next to Bennett, and held the tray on his lap. Bennett was flat on his back, his eyes closed, but when Dad sat down, he put his knees up and sort of bunched himself together. Even though he was wide awake my brother still sounded like he was snoring.

"I feel a little responsible for what happened," Dad began after he asked Bennett how he was feeling. I was on my way down to breakfast when he came in, but decided I didn't want to miss any of this, so I sat down at my desk, put a cough drop in my mouth, and prepared myself for whatever was coming.

"On the other hand, Bennett, when I told you to get rid of the kite, I didn't mean for you to get out of a sickbed and risk your life to do it! Let me tell you, when your mother called me—anyway, you had us all pretty upset."

Bennett's head turned toward Dad, but nothing came out of his mouth. Maybe he was waiting for Dad to let him have it because he'd taken the video camera without permission.

"I understand you've lost your voice." Dad leaned forward and looked at Bennett closely, as if he could see his vocal cords just by peering at his skin. Not a word about the camera.

Bennett didn't shake his head yes or no, just kept looking at Dad and breathing snores.

"You don't have to say anything, son. It's a lucky thing you weren't drowned. I understand you wanted to videotape the kite. It was such a foolhardy thing to do!" Bennett blinked at Dad and Dad sighed. Then he said, "I don't understand how you fell into the water but the camera was still lying on the bridge. I'll never understand why it never even got wet."

This was a question, but Dad didn't put a question mark at the end of it. He just sat looking at Bennett as if he'd never seen him before. Bennett blinked some more, but said nothing. Dad sort of waited. Then he offered Bennett tea and toast, but Bennett shook his head no. Mom had been up earlier with juice and cereal and got the same response. She did get some striped pills into him, though.

"I'll just leave it here for you, Bennett," Dad said, and he got up and put the tray on Bennett's desk.

At the door, he stopped and turned. "You see, son, how lucky that you had all that swim training. It probably saved your life. It's too late this year, but maybe next year, when you're in high school, you'll think about getting back into competitive—" Dad stopped, probably caught the look on Bennett's face and changed his mind about what he was going to say. "We can talk about that later. Look, it's too bad about the kite. Maybe you'll make another one. Bigger, even. I once saw one on TV that looked like a fighter jet. It won a contest. It was sensational. Hey, Bennett, don't look at me like that. Getting rid of that big flying rainbow, well, this is a small town,

Bennett, people talk, it's all yakkity-yak, and, well, you did the right thing, son, the right thing!"

My brother all of a sudden crumpled up in bed and turned his face to the wall. Dad didn't move, but I saw his expression change. He looked totally punched out.

"Your mother," he began, and stopped cold to clear his voice, or just rearrange words in his head, "your mother thinks you, maybe you tried to kill yourself. I told her that was ridiculous; you wouldn't ever do that. Would you?"

I couldn't look at Dad's face anymore. It looked as if it were going to melt. Bennett's back was turned to us and Dad was talking to the back of his head. My brother's hair was all messed up because he'd been lying on it since yesterday. It reminded me of the piles of dead hair you sometimes see on the barbershop floor.

"Listen, son, I'm not telling anybody. *Anybody.* I don't think you should, either. As soon as your voice comes back, we're going to take you to see somebody."

Dad cleared his throat and now addressed me. I was trying not to cough and was just staring at the floor. "Matthew, everything said here stays in this room, okay?"

I said okay and then Dad put his hand on the wall near the door, but didn't slap it. I figured that maybe this was the one time he was glad that Bennett didn't finish what he started to do. "Hey. Is that Mickey Mantle poster new? I like it. I really do," my father said.

40

By the time I got back to school it was obvious that absolutely everyone seemed to know what Bennett had done. It began with Kim passing me a note in math asking if it was true that my brother had tried to drown himself and continued with the principal's secretary stopping me in the hall with a sad face to ask if Bennett was all right and would he be coming to graduation a week from Saturday? I was pretty sure Go-go and his gang were looking at me, waiting to jump in with some disgusting comments, so I steered clear of them as best I could. The weather was warm enough now so I ate my sandwich alone in a spot on the north side of the school yard. I didn't want to run into Nolan or any of his brothers, either.

At first I couldn't imagine how what Dad had called "yakkity-yak" had spread so fast, and then I figured it out: the guy who owned the tackle shop had a kid at our school. That did it. We were suddenly very famous in the worst possible way.

When I got home after my first day back at school after what someone in gym class called Bennett's Brodie, I told my brother what was happening. I figured there'd be some stuff said, whispers, whistles, or who-knows-what-else Go-go and his pals could come up with. Even at graduation.

Bennett wrote me a note:

I AM NOT GOING

"What do you mean, 'not going'? *Miss your own graduation?*"

I thought of Bennett's new shoes and Mom's new dress. I thought about how she'd looked forward to the occasion, how the whole family would be there to hear "We Are the World" and how proud Mom and Dad would be to see Bennett go up on stage and get his diploma. He'd told us he might even get a Science Notable Mention for the special project he did on high-altitude weather balloons. Dad was planning to videotape all the ceremonies. And isn't graduation day one of those red-letter events you're likely to remember until you're too old to remember anything else? How could he even think of not going?

"You have to," I said. "Have to!"

GIVE IT UP

my brother wrote.

I AM QUEER. I BELONG NOWHERE

I was the one with the cough that wouldn't go away, but Bennett swallowed those striped pills and was back on his feet almost immediately. He'd nearly lost his life in the freezing dunk off Edgewater Point, but here he was two days later, all the pink spots gone, looking like an ad for the health benefits of fresh orange juice.

Although not using his vocal cords. Even when his breathing got back to being quiet, when it came to speaking, he'd shut down. He carried a pad around the house and wrote words with his ballpoint pen with the flashlight tip. He'd tied it to a string around his neck like a lariat, and that was that. Bennett had flat-out given up speech.

I got him the homework assignments and Bennett was sitting at the kitchen table most days now, writing term papers and studying for finals. I knew he could have gone to school and so did Mom and Dad, but no one said a thing about it. We all sort of pretended that he was still sick and that's why he was at home. When the school nurse called one day, I heard Mom say, "He hasn't gotten his voice back," which was true—in a way. She said the same thing when Grandma called and wanted to speak to Bennett, to tell him she'd sent him a graduation gift of a U. S. government bond. "He's had the flu and lost his voice," Mom said to Grandma. "He'll call as soon as he can speak."

The way things were going, I thought that would be never.

I could hear Mom and Dad in the bedroom whispering to each other every night. I could hear their voices get angry, upset, and then there'd be long silences or slamming doors. Once Dad left the house before dinner and didn't come back until we had finished helping Mom with the dishes. This time, he hadn't gone out to buy paint.

That's when I went to the window and looked up at the moon myself. It was only half full, and I didn't know what to ask for. I just stood there at the window looking up at the sky and all I said was "Help."

Maybe Bennett believes in conversations with astral bodies, but I don't, but it was the very next day that Shearon came by. One could almost have thought the moon had sent him.

41

I had no idea Shearon was the eyes and ears of our school. He rang the bell just as I was taking my band uniform out of the closet to make sure no buttons were missing, Mom's orders. Dad hadn't come home from work yet, and Mom had run out to pick up a replacement for the gardening gloves she couldn't find. She planned to plant a row of some kind of flowers, I forget which, along the driveway and around the lamppost. She said she was late planting but hoped for the best. Dad and Bennett had repainted the garage doors and she thought the house deserved a pick-me-up. We all did, is what I knew she was thinking.

Bennett came into the kitchen as I was pouring Shearon a glass of Coke. Shearon said he was thirsty, but it turned out he was hungry too. Mom had left a box of doughnut holes in full view and it was hard to miss his eyes going in their direction. "Your mother is some cook." He winked at Bennett.

THEY'RE FROM DUNKIN' DONUTS, my brother wrote on a piece of paper he ripped off a pad Mom has stuck on the refrigerator. He handed the note to Shearon.

"Okay then, she's some shopper." Shearon's mouth was full, he had sugar all over it as he said this, and he proceeded to laugh for about five minutes. Then he asked Bennett why he wasn't talking.

MY VOICE GONE,

Bennett wrote. As soon as he was finished, he put the ballpoint-pen-on-a-string back around his neck.

"Gone where? Fishing?" Shearon laughed for like another five minutes. Bennett didn't even smile. "Who you kidding?" Shearon wanted to know. Bennett glared at him.

"I bet there's nothing wrong with your vocal cords. You just don't want to talk, that's all." Shearon turned to me. "Got any more soda in that cold box, Matthew?"

I went to the refrigerator to see what I could find. "We only have root beer," I said.

Shearon said he was okay with that and he liked it with lots of ice. I poured some in a glass and Shearon wanted to know if we had any straws. "I have sensitive teeth," he said.

Bennett was sitting at the kitchen table with his arms crossed over his shirt and an I-don't-believe-this look on his face.

I was surprised too. On the other hand, you never knew what to expect from Shearon. "You know what, Bennett, you need some reality orientation," he said, which was a thought that seemed not to follow the drift of the current conversation. "Although, what I really came over for was my dolly. I need it to move some stuff for my dad."

I found a straw and gave it to Shearon, and he stuck it in his root beer and drank practically half. Then he said, "I mean, it's not my job to get you to say something. Your voice going on strike is a cop-out, that's what I think. Bad enough you screwed up the swim team's chance for the regional championship."

I quick looked at my brother to see his reaction, but he was frozen there with his arms crossed, except for his Adam's apple, which went up and down a couple of times.

"You know, pal, you better learn to roll with the punches. Although, I admit I thought of doing myself in once or twice too," Shearon said between taking sips through his straw and looking down into his root beer. I figured he didn't want to look right at Bennett, and neither did I. It seemed a very bad time to get my brother fired up. "You know, Bennett, you being food for the fishes, that would have been one bad scene. As it is, the whole school got a lecture and a forty-minute movie in assembly about teenage suicide. It cut right into my gym class too." Shearon looked up at Bennett then. "And I had to miss *volleyball*—Although it was a good movie, Bennett. You should've been there. See, putting yourself out of misery puts everybody else into it, that was the gist. In other words, like your swim team caper, it's not only about *you*."

Bennett was sitting there like a statue in the park. It was not enough he'd given up talking. Now he looked like he'd given up inhaling and exhaling.

I guessed they showed the movie the day I was home coughing and was annoyed that I missed something I shouldn't have missed!

Bennett leaned over the table then, took his ballpoint pen from around his neck and began writing. I looked to see what the note said when Shearon picked it up.

THE DOLLY IS IN THE GARAGE

Shearon said, "As soon as I finish the soda, I'll get it," but then, he stopped sipping. "I was the only black kid in my whole third-, fourth-, and fifth-grade classes until the Ashley kids moved to my neighborhood. If some kid refused to come to my house after school, I never knew if it was cause they really had to go home to do homework or wouldn't come over cause I was black. I was always reading the environment, if you know what I mean, and I bet you do. And I still do read people's faces and voices, a copious amount of the time. 'Copious' is an eighth-grade vocabulary word, by the way."

Bennett's face was not readable, but he was listening.

"And you know what else? When my mother tried to sign me up to take ballroom dancing at the Willard Dance Studio, they didn't have room for me. A week later three kids in my fifth-grade class got accepted. And, of course, everybody knew they were desperate for boys! Want to hear more, Ben-boy? I once got arrested for jaywalking. Jaywalking! Ever hear anybody get taken to the police station for jaywalking? My dad had to hire a lawyer, and guess what? He hired a white one, just to make sure I'd get my name erased from the police blotter!"

Bennett took his ballpoint pen from around his neck again. He was writing a mile a minute.

YOUR FAMILY IS MEMBER OF SAME MINORITY AS YOU. YOU'RE IN IT TOGETHER

"Hey, well, you got a point there. But so, it's about your family too. And think of your little brother here, although I know he's sometimes a pain in the butt. He'd never get over it if you took yourself out. And you really want to do that to your mom and dad? Grief counseling and cemetery visits and guilt forever? You should've seen that movie!"

"Why am I a pain in the butt?" I asked Shearon, who ignored me and kept addressing Bennett, who took a quick glance at me. He reached over and grabbed a doughnut hole and took a bite. Now at least his eyes were moving.

"And you got friends." Shearon was making sucking noises with his straw. He'd finally gone back to finishing his soda.

Bennett shook his head. He pulled his pen from around his neck and wrote

I HAVE NO FRIENDS

"You'd be surprised," Shearon said, and he took a doughnut hole out of the box and threw it at Bennett. Bennett ducked and it hit a cupboard and fell on the floor. "And if you promise to come to graduation, I'll give you some really good news."

Bennett seemed to come alive, but just for a second. He shook his head no.

"Hey, stay home then. All I can say is, if I were you I'd go. The fat lady's gonna sing."

Bennett picked up a doughnut hole and tossed it at the ceiling, then caught it on the way down. He popped it into his mouth, ate it, and burped in two keys, while Shearon and I watched him.

Shearon got up, gave me a high five, took a last doughnut hole himself. "The dolly's in the garage, right?" he said, and he stopped at the basement door and shook his head. "Anyway, the principal is going to talk about hate crimes at graduation. His secretary told me to tell you. And you aren't going to be there. You'd rather sit here like a big fat sphinx!"

Shearon was pointing at Bennett with his two pointer fingers held out under his chin like a pair of guns. "You know what, Bennett? If people don't like you, hey, it's *their* problem, not yours, so GET OVER IT!" Then he thanked me for the soda and refreshments and popped the doughnut hole into his mouth before disappearing down the basement stairs.

42

If you think that Shearon changed Bennett's mind, think again. Even the call that came later from the school principal, who assured Bennett of a diploma and excused him from finals until after the graduation ceremonies because of his good grades, didn't soften him up. Day of graduation, Dad made his usual Saturday cinnamon toast and piled it high on Bennett's plate with a big strawberry on top, and Mom put a card in front of his plate that said "Congratulations." As soon as we finished eating, Mom and Dad gave Bennett his graduation present, the Palm Pilot he's been wanting since the Christmas before last. Bennett wrote,

THANK YOU THANK YOU

on a paper napkin, but not a word came out of his mouth. I felt pretty guilty not to have bought my brother a present but with everything happening in the last week or so, I'd just forgotten all about doing it. Now he was still sitting at the kitchen table in his bathrobe, his mouth buttoned up, when Mom and Dad were getting ready to drive me to the school.

I was waiting in the doorway, stuffed into my band uniform, which was itchy around the neck and too tight in the shoulders, wanting to get to the gym early, but no. Mom and Dad were hovering over my brother, still hoping he'd change his mind.

"You know, Bennett, graduation is called 'commencement.' Do you know what 'commencement' means?" Dad was saying.

Bennett had the Palm Pilot in his hand and was giving it his full attention. He was in his own zone and didn't seem to have heard Dad.

"It means 'to begin.' That's what it means. Maybe if you think of it as a new start, you might," Dad continued before Bennett could shake his head yes or no, ". . . you might look at things in another light. You'll be going off to the high school in a few months and things will be very different—"

Just as he was going to launch into a new version of We Must Strive, the doorbell rang. Even before I knew who was at the door, I was glad for the interruption. It was pretty hot today, and now the band uniform felt as if it had shrunk a size just since I put it on. Even my shoes felt tight.

"Valerie! Gretchen!" I heard Mom at the door, and a minute later, into the kitchen they both came, Valerie first. I swear, when I saw what she was carrying, I nearly dropped my saxophone case.

"His name is Leonardo. We named him after Valerie's favorite artist. Someone found the poor thing wandering on the highway and brought him to our vet. So there he was when we picked up Blanche and, bingo! I suddenly remembered Bennett. Aren't you graduating today, Bennett? How's this for a nice graduation present?" That was Gretchen, who had followed Valerie in and seemed to be doing all the talking today.

"Your Mom and Dad said it was all right if you want to keep him. He's only three months old."

I figured this was all a setup, a *conspiracy* (a sixth-grade vocabulary word) and I loved it!

Bennett put down his Palm Pilot and his eyes got so big they looked like they were going to roll right out of his head. Actually, I'll bet my eyes were bugging out too. The fact is, I nearly stopped breathing because I was really scared Bennett would say that no way was Leonardo going to replace Frankie. Even if my brother didn't want this puppy, I did! It had a black body and a white chest and looked just like a small version of a big dog I saw stealing a kid's lunch in a TV commercial.

But my brother still said nothing. Just sat there, while a silence bunched up like steam in our kitchen. "Don't you want to at least pet him?" Mom asked. I saw Dad out of the corner of my eye and he was rubbing his bad shoulder. I wondered if it was really hurting or just the fidgets; he seemed awfully quiet, for Dad. Finally, Bennett slowly got up, walked over to Valerie, and patted Leonardo on the head. I wished Valerie's vet had found a dog with one ear up and one down, but both the puppy's ears were flapped down and there was no telling what the future of either one was going to be.

"We thought we'd surprise you, but you can keep him on approval, like sort of a trial run," Valerie said, and now it seemed like it was her turn to talk. "He's paper trained. He's friendly and loves to have his head scratched. He's afraid of thunder and lightning, and loves to chase squirrels. And the most unusual thing about Leonardo is that he has six toes on each paw. The vet says that's really unusual. See, little Leo is a bit unique!"

"Well, aren't we all!" Mom said then, and if ever there was a loaded earful, that was it. I practically heard the follow-up no one actually said: *it's okay to be different*, but if the message sunk in with Bennett, he gave no sign. He was too busy counting Leonardo's toes, and not saying boo. I was feeling hopeful, but there was no more time to feel anything; now it was really time to leave.

The surprise is that Bennett did finally go to graduation, but I don't think it was the puppy that got my brother to change his mind. I think what happened was that Valerie let him hold Leo, and when he had the puppy in his arms and the sleeves of his robe curled around its little body, he looked up and just happened to catch the expression on Mom's face. She was looking at him, her head was bent just a little bit to the side, and I'm sure he saw what I did: her face was soft and sad and it said, *Please don't let me down*, and when she took a step towards my brother, it was clear as anything that it also had *I love you mucho-mucho* written all over it.

43

Maybe what happened at graduation should have made the papers, but it never did. And who knows but my brother might have permanently been speechless, if he hadn't decided at the last minute to put on his new shoes, throw on his cap and gown, and make Mom and Dad happy by going. The way things were spinning out, I was afraid he'd lose the use of his vocal cords just because he'd gone so long without using them. Now that I've given it a lot of thought, I imagine he'd shut down and shut up so he wouldn't have to talk to the "someone" Dad wanted to send him to to make him stop being gay.

Dad never weighed in when Mom said it was okay to be "different" and for Bennett, I think Dad's talks sometimes sounded like knock-downs. Not that my father said it in so many words, but he made my brother feel like he had to hide behind a fake Bennett to measure up. Sometimes Mom stood up to Dad, but other times she sort of got quiet in the interests of home peace. What was Bennett thinking? Friends gone, kite gone, with Dad's heart often in the wrong place, well, like my brother said to Shearon, he got the idea even having his family behind him wasn't a sure thing.

I got to school just in the nick of time. Seats were lined up on the football field, the bleachers were full and the band marched in playing Sousa. By this time I knew that march so well I never made one mistake, and felt pretty good about myself. Then, *The Star Spangled Banner*, which is a no-brainer I learned long ago. The band sat at the back of the stage, and before the ceremony began, two of the band members played solos, but I'm not good enough, so I was just sitting back there, waiting through them and wondering how I was going to put a knot in my right shoelace, which had come untied.

The principal got up to speak and I was watching the back of his head when he began, focusing on this round bald patch I'd never really noticed before. While he was going on about the future of America being in the hands of the graduates of Clara Barton Junior High and naming famous graduates I'd never heard of, my mind was wandering. Every so often I checked the audience looking for my brother, and finally found him sitting in the second row of blue caps and gowns, with Jeremy and Shearon a row behind him. His face looked like it had in the kitchen: blah.

The sun was really beaming down and it was in my eyes, which explains why I couldn't easily find Mom and Dad. Basically, I was focused on my shoelace and Kim Yee, who was just getting up to blow into her baritone sax. Her solo was something real forgettable from an opera I never heard of. When she finished, after the applause died down, she turned to go back to her seat and gave me a big smile with her new teeth. I thought I might ask her to come watch me play softball next week.

I finally found my parents in the audience, saw them sitting on the aisle about four rows back. I wished I could wave to cheer them up because even though Dad would now get his video of Bennett getting his diploma (which I knew he wanted to send to Grandma and Grandpa) my parents looked pretty run down. I also wished I could get out of my band uniform, which was now squeezing me in some places and making me itchy in others.

The principal went on and on, but things were picking up. He started talking about hate crimes and how hateful they are, and how we should all pretend we're cousins, no matter how different we are from each other, and then saying that something "outrageous" had happened in our very own community. He said he was sure no one would condone "malicious" behavior towards any minority. He was pretty excited by this time and I knew he was talking about Bennett, so I began listening with all my ear cells. Without mentioning his name, he talked about Go-go. He said "the perpetrators" had been "apprehended stealing spray paint, had confessed to engaging in spraying hate graffiti," and would be sentenced in juvenile court, there given appropriate punishment. *Punishment!* It was a word more beautiful than music, more delicious than brownies! It was a word with a 14-karat gold halo! Like Shearon said, the fat lady was going to sing! I knew he wouldn't be locked up with murderers or whipped with chains, but I guessed I wouldn't be seeing much of Go-go in school for a while!

I checked Bennett's face to see if the word *punishment* had registered, but there was no change. Wasn't he *listening*?

Then the principal said something that really hit me like a hammer. I was sure it would stick in my head forever, and I guess it was another quote, maybe from another century, from some very smart, very dead author. It was beautiful, it was perfect, the way it applied to Go-go. "All cruelty comes from weakness," the principal said and I was mega sorry Go-go wasn't here to hear it. I did spot a few amigos in the audience, but didn't trust them to carry the word. I promised myself to go to the computer as soon as I got home, type out "All cruelty comes from weakness" in big letters in Bennett's favorite font, Arial Black, and stick it in Go-go's locker. My contribution: sooner or later, one way or another—maybe it was wishful thinking—I hoped Go-go Mallis and all his buddies would get the message.

My brother never did get the Science Award for high altitude weather balloons. Actually, Terry, the new kid, got it for his forest fire prevention exhibit. He also got an award in English Poetry and one for General Excellence. All this time we never knew we had a brain living next door.

But even if he was disappointed not to get a science award, I think what Bennett got was greater than all the other prizes lumped together.

What happened was that the principal had a whole bunch of diplomas with ribbons in a big basket and started calling names of graduates in alphabetical order. Every time he called a name and a cap and gown walked on stage and was given a handshake and one of the rolled-up diplomas, the audience let out a cheer. Some were loud cheers and some were not so loud—like for an amigo generally hated by one and all, or for someone new to the school or just one of the known dorks—and then

Bennett's name was called. I didn't know what was coming, whether there'd be a total silence or boos or just a little polite applause, but what I didn't expect was this amazing explosion.

What burst out was not only cheers, whistles, and foot stomps but then—Dad got it all on videotape—Jeremy leaped up, pulled off his cap, and his hair was striped in rainbow colors! And now the triplets came running down the aisle yelling and waving their baseball caps and, you guessed it, their hair was dyed in the same rainbow stripes! All of a sudden I saw a whole bunch of kids pull off their graduation caps or just appear from the back of the audience, and they'd done it too. They'd dyed their hair in reds and greens and blues, not exactly Roy G. Biv, but in that spirit. It was an amazing, dazzling, eye-popping, once-in-a-lifetime sight. One for the books, is how Mom later put it.

Now it was me that felt as if I'd lost my voice. I was definitely speechless, not that anyone had asked me to make one. My brother, the star! Well, maybe it was really my brother, the symbol, which is what the principal explained.

When Bennett walked up onto the stage, he gave him his diploma and a hug. "I think your fellow graduates and the students of Clara Barton want to make it all up to you," the principal said, and there was another loud cheer. "You've become an emblem of our tolerance and we want you to know we're sorry for what you've had to go through," he continued. Someone yelled, "BENN-NETT! BENN-NETT!" and more kids picked it up: "BENN-NETT! BENN-NETT!" was all you could hear, loud and louder. My brother looked boggled. He shook the principal's hand and I heard his first words come squeaking out of his mouth: "Thank you, sir," he said.

I looked at my parents and saw that Dad had put down his video camera and taken out his handkerchief. He took off the sunglasses we'd given him and was wiping his eyes. Mom had jumped up to applaud, and I saw Dad reach up and hand it to her so she could wipe hers too. All this time there was whistling, stomping and cheering and when my brother stepped off the stage, he was surrounded by a rainbow of hair. Shearon's too! I guessed he was the one who'd put everyone up to it, probably with the help of Jeremy's sister. There she was, with a red-yellow-green-and-blue head of hair, giving Bennett a high five. I put two and two together and decided that maybe the dolly isn't the only reason Shearon had come by yesterday.

All I remember of the rest of that graduation ceremony is "We Are the World," which we played after all the diplomas had been handed out. I made at least three mistakes, but no one (except of course the band teacher) noticed. While I was blowing my notes, I thought about the rainbow kite, how I'd seen it sailing away in the sky. Maybe someday Bennett would build another one; then again, maybe he wouldn't. Some things are just one-shot, and the kite might have been one of them. Anyway, I was sure that all the rainbows here today would make better history. It was the kind of memory that would never sail away into the sky, but would stay stuck in all our heads forever.

And on tape, like the kite, in Dad's video camera.

After the ceremonies, Dad took us out to a Chinese restaurant to celebrate. I thought that my father's heart would finally slide into the right place, just by the way he kept his arm around Bennett while he told us that Leonardo daVinci was one of the greatest artists of all time. "He was gay too," Dad said. His eyes had red rims, but he was smiling. And Bennett's voice was back full steam. He ordered Lo Mein, Crispy Orange Duck and brown rice. He also wanted two Cokes and a side of dumplings. I don't remember what message came out of his fortune cookies, but I remember mine: "It is certain you will not soon again shed tears." I handed it to Bennett and he read it and stuck it in his pocket.

"If you walk him in the morning, I'll walk him at night," he said.

"I'll buy the leash," I told him. "It'll be your graduation present, okay?"

"Okay," Bennett said, and then he burped in two keys. When both Mom and Dad gave him looks, it seemed like things were pretty much back to normal in our family.